Suffering in silence

Mac touched his arm gently, and Jamey winced, but when Mac pushed up his sleeve to examine the small scrape on his elbow, Jamey gazed at it, too, with apparent interest.

"I think we could use a Band-Aid on this," Mac said. "Let's see your side."

Jamey shook his head. "It's okay."

But Mac had already reached to pull up both the orange T-ball shirt and the white tee shirt underneath.

Lauri leaned forward, then paused, shocked by what she saw. Several long yellowish bruises showed on Jamey's skinny little torso . . .

LIFE AT SIXTEEN
Silent Tears

Cheryl Zach

BERKLEY JAM BOOKS, NEW YORK

SILENT TEARS

A Berkley Jam Book / published by arrangement with
the author

PRINTING HISTORY
Berkley Jam edition / February 1999

The Penguin Putnam Inc. World Wide Web site address is
http://www.penguinputnam.com

ISBN: 0-425-16739-9

BERKLEY JAM BOOKS®
Berkley Jam Books are published by The Berkley Publishing Group,
a division of Penguin Putnam Inc.,
375 Hudson Street, New York, New York 10014.
BERKLEY JAM and its logo are trademarks
belonging to Penguin Putnam Inc.

PRINTED IN THE UNITED STATES OF AMERICA

10 9 8 7 6 5 4 3

*For Tracy, Mary, Nancy, Thea, and Cheryl M.,
with thanks for all your helpful comments and
loyal support*

CHAPTER ONE

"We're going to lose our house!" Marietta Whitley announced, her voice heavy with impending doom. "We'll probably be walking the streets and living out of a grocery cart, next!" She ran one hand through her artfully tinted auburn hair and sighed heavily.

Sixteen-year-old Lauri Whitley looked at her mother and shook her head. A lock of her own naturally brown hair fell into her face, and she pushed it back. "Mom, you say that every month when it's time to pay the bills. You're overreacting."

Her mother picked up a statement and waved it in the air, her tone still shrill. "No, I'm not. The mortgage payment is so big—I just can't keep up. And there's the electric and gas bills, and the car payment, and we have to eat. Ever since the divorce—if Roy had agreed to a better settlement . . ."

"You wanted the house, he gave you the house." Lauri glanced around the living room of the comfortable ranch house now occupied by only her and her mother.

Her stepfather had moved out over a year ago. Would they really have to give up their home, or was it just her mom having another tantrum?

She thought of her familiar blue and white bedroom with her white wicker-frame bed and her favorite rock star posters on the wall and tried to repress a tremor of fear. Where would they go? She had a sudden vision of her mother and her on the street, shivering in the rain, and pushed it aside. She couldn't panic, too.

"But I didn't realize—on one income, I just can't keep up. Roy made so much more than I do." Her mother frowned and tossed the bills back onto the table.

"You want me to quit school? High school dropouts don't make that much, but . . ." Lauri wrapped the sarcasm around herself, a defense against the very real fear that her mother's words evoked. But her mother always fussed about money. It couldn't really be that bad, could it?

To her shock, she watched her mother's blue eyes fill with tears. "It's not a joke!" Her mother snapped, putting one hand up to hide her face. "It's really bad this time, Lauri. I didn't want to tell you, but I just can't keep up, and I don't know where to turn."

The fear inside her grew, cold and heavy. Lauri still didn't want to believe it. "So, we'll cut back," she said, her voice uncertain, trying to bluff her way past the anxiety that churned inside her stomach. "We'll eat beans and rice, and—and we could drop the extra channels on the cable, that would save money, wouldn't it? And—"

"Lauri, I can't pay the mortgage; it's not just a dollar here or there," her mother repeated. "I'm not making enough to pay the bills." The desperation in her voice made Lauri grow cold inside.

She looked at her mom, wanting to protest again, but this time her mother gazed back, meeting her eyes. Was it really true?

"What will we do?" Lauri almost whispered.

Her mother shook her head. "I don't know," she said, sounding so defeated that the coldness inside Lauri spread even further. "I just don't know. If Roy hadn't left . . ."

It was always a man that her mother looked to to save them, Lauri thought. Another man, another marriage, and eventually, more loud arguments, another divorce. She shivered at the memories.

"If your dad was paying his child support, if I even knew where he was so I could try to make him pay . . ." Her mother sighed again.

Lauri shrugged away the discomfort that mention of her father evoked. She hadn't seen her dad in years; he had stopped sending checks or calling her on birthdays or holidays soon after the divorce. Obviously, he didn't care what happened to his daughter. Did he even remember her? That thought was too painful. She didn't care, Lauri told herself stubbornly. Who cared, anyhow?

She reached tentatively toward her mother, wanting to touch her, to ease the worry in her face. But her mother had turned away and didn't seem to see the motion.

"We always make it, somehow," Lauri told her mom, trying to offer some comfort.

The doorbell rang, and Lauri stifled a sigh of relief. She wanted out of the house, away from the tension that gripped her stomach and turned it inside out. "That's Karen; I'm eating dinner at her house, remember."

Her mother grimaced. "Oh, sure, you leave, too!"

Lauri winced. "I'll stay home if you want," she said. "Karen asked me last week to come for dinner because we have a school project to finish, but—"

"Oh, go on." Her mother waved her hand. "What difference does it make? I'm used to being alone. Anyhow, it's free food."

Lauri bit her lip, glad that her best friend was not able to hear the bitter remark. The bell chimed again.

"You sure?" she asked.

Her mother nodded, her face twisted with self-pity.

Lauri didn't know what else to say. Her mother was supposed to be the grown-up; Lauri didn't know how to help her. And she really wanted to get away from the house, heavy with its atmosphere of worry. But she looked at her mom one more time before turning toward the door—she looked so alone. "Why don't you call one of your friends?"

"Jean is in Mexico for two weeks, and Sandra's gone back east to see her new grandbaby," her mother said, once more running one hand through her hair.

"Call Uncle Jack," Lauri suggested. "He's divorced, too; he should understand how you feel. He might even have some ideas about the house and the budget."

Her mother nodded, her frown easing slightly. "Maybe I will. You be home by nine."

Lauri picked up her backpack and met her friend at the door.

"Hi," Karen said. She was a sun-streaked blonde, two inches shorter and somewhat more rounded than Lauri, and her easy grin was a relief after the swirling currents of discontent that seemed to fill the Whitley home.

"Let's go," Lauri said, almost pushing her best friend back across the threshold. "Bye, Mom," she called over her shoulder. "I'll be home early."

When she had shut the door firmly behind them, they walked down to the sidewalk. The California sun shone brightly, and the air was balmy. Santa Clarissa was a middle-class neighborhood within commuting distance of Los Angeles, and Lauri and her mom had lived here for over three years—a record so far. Lauri thought about the local high school, where she had friends, where she knew people, about Karen, and the coldness came back.

"What's going on?" Karen asked. "Your mom having a bad day again?"

"The worst," Lauri said, her shoulders still tight with tension. "Mom is freaking out, saying we're going to lose our house, that she can't pay all the bills by herself."

"That's bad," Karen agreed, her usual cheerful grin fading.

"She's worried about money before, but I thought she was exaggerating," Lauri told her best friend. "I hope it's not true; I don't want to lose our house! You'd think she'd have done a better job of the divorce, I mean, she's had enough practice."

"How many is it this time?" Karen glanced at her curiously. "Three, four?"

"Four."

"It doesn't bother you?"

Lauri kicked at a rock on the sidewalk. "No, not much. Roy wasn't my dad, you know. *He* left a long time ago." But even she could hear the bitterness in her voice.

"You wouldn't have to move—far, I mean?" Karen looked alarmed. "I mean, we're going to have a great year—we're not freshmen any more, and we're both in Mr. Dugan's psych class, which is the most interesting class we've ever had, and there's the homecoming dance coming up—we have all these plans!"

"I know," Lauri said. "We can't move; we just can't. I hope it's just my mom having one of her panic attacks. Come on, let's go to your house and forget this for a while."

Karen nodded. "You want to hang out at the mall for an hour or two, first?"

"No point, I'm broker than broke." Lauri shifted her backpack to the other shoulder. "Let's go tackle that psych project and then put a movie into the VCR— something funny, with no divorces and nobody worrying about money."

"Right," Karen agreed.

Two hours later, they finished the psych paper they were doing jointly and left the printer humming as it printed out the three copies their teacher had requested. Karen's mother called them to dinner, and Lauri sat down to the big round dining table and glanced around her. She loved being here; if only Lauri didn't have to move away from her friend!

"Hurry up with the chicken," Karen's ten-year-old brother Martin begged. "I'm starving."

"Coming." Karen's mom passed the platter to Lauri. "Guests first, Martin."

Lauri selected a piece of chicken and put it on her plate, then passed the platter on, grinning at the little boy.

"No broccoli," Karen's six-year-old sister Angie said, wrinkling her nose. "I hate broccoli!"

"Just a spoonful," her mother suggested.

Angie shook her head, her small round face distorted into a grimace. "I really, really hate broccoli," she said darkly.

"If Angie ate a piece of broccoli, the roof might fall in," Karen's dad suggested, his tone teasing.

"Yeah, right," Martin muttered.

"Really?" Angie asked, her eyes bright.

Their father glanced up at the ceiling with exaggerated concern. "I wouldn't take any bets."

"Maybe just a little tiny spoonful." Angie looked from the ceiling back to the table, obviously intrigued.

The family's big collie nudged Lauri's leg, and she glanced at him, her forkful of chicken momentarily arrested in midair. "Nope, Tramp, no handouts."

Angie took a bite of broccoli, made a face, but chewed and swallowed. "See, the roof didn't fall," she said, waving her hand and knocking over her glass of milk.

Mrs. Karensky jumped up and came back with paper towels, while Martin laughed and Angie wailed.

Karen glanced at Lauri and frowned in embarrassment. "Sorry."

"Don't be, I like it," Lauri told her friend, thinking of the silent, often tense dinners she shared with her mom at home. She enjoyed the cheerful chaos of Karen's house. Too bad her mother couldn't stay married long enough to have more kids, Lauri thought. It would have been nice to have laughter and teasing conversations, not sullen silences or loud quarrels that killed her appetite and sent her hurrying away from the dinner table while the adults traded barbs with each other.

Lauri thought of her mom's last two marriages, the only ones she could remember well, and sighed again. Her own father had been a systems analyst for an international oil company, and she wasn't even sure where he was living now; the last time she'd heard from him was two years ago. He'd been in Venezuela, that time. She pushed the old hurt away and watched, grinning, as Angie took one more bite of broccoli.

After dinner, she and Karen cleared the table and loaded the dishwasher, then Karen led them back to her bedroom and shut the door firmly. "My family!" she muttered.

"I love your family," Lauri told her. "They're like a sitcom."

"This is good?" Karen demanded. "Easy for you to say. What, they make you laugh?"

"Yes, no, I mean, they have disagreements, but it's all cleared up in thirty minutes, that sort of thing. I wish I knew how they do it. I wish my mom knew!"

Karen nodded. "Yeah, I guess that's rough."

Her look of sympathy suddenly made Lauri want to change the subject. "So, what are you wearing to the homecoming dance?"

"Oh, my mom finally said I could get a new dress," Karen bounced on her bed with excitement. "Will you come with us when we go to the mall to look? I just wish you were going to the dance, too. Why did you break up with David? He's pretty cute, and he liked you."

"You know." Lauri picked up one of the stuffed animals that covered Karen's bed and stroked the elephant's soft plush. "He was putting the moves on Sherri Lancaster."

"You don't really know that," Karen objected. "Just because he sat beside her at lunch one day—"

"Oh, leave it," Lauri said, suddenly irritated. "Let's talk about your love life, not mine, okay?"

"Okay," Karen agreed. "Let me show you a dress I saw in a magazine ad."

While she flipped through the pages of a teen magazine, Lauri looked around the cheerful yellow bedroom and thought about Karen's family and Karen's house, its slightly shabby furnishings and the cheerful flowers in the overgrown flowerbeds outside. The house Karen had no worries about losing. . . .

When Lauri walked home in the soft September darkness, hurrying past the street lights till she could turn into her own street, Lauri wondered what kind of mood her mom would be in. Hopefully, the worst of her anxiety would have passed, and there would be no more dire warnings about being out on the street. Just thinking about that possibility made Lauri's stomach tighten into hard knots. When her mother was obsessing about money, Lauri couldn't sleep at night, sometimes.

Stay cool, she told herself as she unlocked the front door and let herself in. The house was quiet, a good sign, and she found her mom sitting on the flowered couch in the living room, flipping through a glossy magazine.

"I'm home," Lauri said cautiously, trying to gage her mom's mood.

Her mother looked up. "Good. Did you get the schoolwork done?"

"Yeah, we should get an A this time, for sure," Lauri predicted, letting her backpack slide to the floor. "You okay?"

Her mom smiled unexpectedly. "Fine. I called Uncle

Jack, and he's going to give me a loan, so that will get us through this month, anyhow. And, Lauri . . .'' she sounded suddenly and unexpectedly nervous, and she looked down at the pages of the magazine, as if not wanting to meet her daughter's eyes.

''What?'' Lauri demanded.

''I got you a job.''

CHAPTER TWO

"What?" Lauri squeaked, then swallowed and managed a more normal tone. "What are you talking about? What kind of job? You don't really expect me to leave school?" She felt as if she had walked into a wall; her knees felt wobbly.

"Of course not," her mother said quickly. "Only after school, silly. I mean, I knew you'd want to help, and since Uncle Jack has been so good . . ."

Lauri dropped into the pink armchair, relieved but still feeling hollow inside. "What does this have to do with Uncle Jack?"

"He needs someone to look after little Jamey after school, and since he's been so good to us . . ." Her mother met her gaze this time, but she bit her lip, looking anxious.

Baby-sitting—oh, great. Lauri's first reaction was resentment—how much would this reduce her free time with Karen and her other friends? But then she thought of her mom's drawn face every month when she struggled with the household bills, and her repeated worries about losing their home.

Lauri took a deep breath, her chest suddenly free of its invisible bands, realizing only now how tense she had been for the last few weeks. She rubbed her fingers absently over the worn plush of the armchair—this chair had been around since before they'd bought the house. They'd had it at the last apartment, and the condo before that, when her mom was still married to Dean. Lauri liked the chair; it felt soft like a teddy bear, and when she was little, she'd often curl up in it when she came home after school and her mom was still at work. She knew about coming home to an empty house.

"I haven't done that much baby-sitting," Lauri said, but she could hear the resignation in her own voice. "I'm not exactly an expert."

"It's not that hard, Lauri, really." Her mother's expression lightened. "You've helped Karen with her little brother and sister."

"I was there when Karen baby-sat; I didn't really do anything," Lauri argued. "I guess I can ask Karen for a crash course in what to with little kids. How old is he now, anyhow?" She frowned trying to remember. "Five, six?"

"He's in first grade," her mother said. "Six, I think. Tomorrow you can walk over to the elementary school after your last class, walk him to the apartment, and wait for Jack to get home from work, that's all. You'll do it?"

She sounded anxious again, and Lauri pushed her own feelings back. She walked over and sat down beside her mother, giving her an impulsive hug.

"Sure."

Her mother put one arm around her shoulders. "Thank goodness. This will be a lifesaver. Besides, it will be good for you to get to know your cousin; they've lived out of state so much since Jamey was born, you hardly know him."

Lauri nodded. "Sure," she agreed, though she felt little enthusiasm for this new family togetherness idea. "What happened to Jamey's mom, anyhow? How come she went off and left her own kid?" At least her mother had stuck around, Lauri thought, even if her dad hadn't. Poor Jamey—left with one parent, just like Lauri.

Her mother shook her head. "I don't really know; she was just a kid herself when they married—maybe she wasn't ready for the responsibility. Being a parent isn't easy."

Lauri hugged her mom again. At least her mom had stayed, she told herself again, fiercely. It was just the two of them—for most of her life, that was how it had been. Of course Lauri had to contribute if she could.

"It'll probably be fun, baby-sitting Jamey," she said, not believing it, but wanting to make the worry lines in her mom's forehead fade.

Her mother's expression lightened. "Good! I knew you'd want to help. Like some ice cream? I've got your favorite pralines and cream in the freezer; we can share it."

Lauri nodded and followed her mom into the kitchen, happy to see her more relaxed than she'd been in months. If this eased her mom's fears, they would both benefit. How bad could it be—watching one six-year-old for a few hours a day? Her own spirits lifting, too, she opened the cabinet to find two bowls while her mother took out a pint of ice cream.

• • •

"Just one?" Karen said the next morning at school, echoing Lauri's thought. "How hard can that be? Good thing your uncle didn't have three or four kids."

Lauri laughed. "I don't think his wife hung around long enough to have more than one. She split when Jamey was only a few months old."

"Geez, really? How could she leave her own little baby?" Karen demanded, pulling books out of the locker.

Lauri shrugged. "I don't know much about it. They were living in Arizona then. I've only seen Jack and little Jamey once since they moved back to southern California, and that was at my grandmother's house."

"Still, that's sort of weird," Karen argued. "Maybe I'll walk over to the elementary school with you. I can collect my own two brats. Now that's a baby-sitting job, I can tell you." Karen slammed the locker door shut just as the warning bell rang. "Yikes, got to run. If I see David, any messages?" she asked, her tone mischievous.

"Tell him to enjoy his lunch with Sherri," Lauri said drily. "See you in psych class." She shifted her backpack to the other shoulder and turned up the hall.

After school, she waited for Karen at the side door, then they walked the mile and a half to the elementary school. Fortunately, the high school started and let out a half hour before the elementary school, so they didn't have to rush. When they reached the low-built multiwinged stucco school building, Lauri paused to get her bearings. She glanced at the note her mom had given her. "Room 12," she told her best friend.

"This way," Karen said. The shrill sound of the bell heralded a sudden rush of feet. "Look out, here they come, the little monsters."

The school was composed of three long wings connected by open-air, roofed walkways, with a central building that Lauri knew from her own elementary school years usually housed offices and a cafeteria.

She hurried her steps—she didn't want Jamey to think she wasn't coming—and pushed through a sudden crowd of small bodies. The little kids shrieked and yelled to each other, and Lauri got banged by a passing lunchbox.

"Ouch," she said, rubbing her elbow.

"Hey, Martin," Karen yelled over the heads of the smaller children. "Wait up."

Karen's brother dropped the kickball he'd been about to toss back to a friend. "What are you doing here? Did Angie tell on me?"

"What is there to tell?" Karen demanded, stepping around a clump of giggling little girls.

"Just because I pulled her hair one time . . ." Martin looked aggrieved.

"Brat!" Karen told him, without heat. "Find Angie and wait for me on the playground; I'll walk home with you guys. And no hair-pulling."

Lauri walked ahead of them and at last located Room 12. She hoped she would recognize Jamey; all these little kids, with their jeans and tee shirts, were a rainbow of black and blonde and red and brown heads, but at the same time, so many of the little boys seemed to look alike. She had seen Jamey only once, and that was at a family dinner. Her aunt Paula's three kids had been loud and noisy and had drawn her eye much more than Jamey, who'd seemed rather quiet, maybe shy. She tried to form a picture of him from her memory and could only call up a vague image of a skinny little boy with sandy brown hair.

She looked inside the classroom. Most of the kids had already hurried out, some walking toward the street where a line of cars sat, each with a parent waiting to pick up children, others heading for the playground. The teacher bent over a small girl with a tearful face, inspecting a scratched finger. But in the back of the room, one small boy lingered at his desk, carefully placing a sheet of paper into his pint-sized backpack.

"Jamey?" Lauri asked, walking closer.

He looked up at her, brown eyes big in a narrow face. She thought his expression looked anxious. He was almost painfully thin, his shoulders narrow beneath a name-brand tee shirt, his jeans and athletic shoes also new and expensive. Did he recognize her?

"It's Lauri, your cousin. Do you remember me from Gramma's house?"

He nodded slowly. "I remember."

"I'm going to walk you back to your apartment, okay?" Lauri smiled at him, trying to put him more at ease. He was so slight of build; she had forgotten how little first graders could be.

The teacher walked back, a Band-Aid in one hand. "Everything all right, Jamey?"

He nodded. "This is my cousin Lauri," he told the teacher. "She's going to baby-sit me after school."

Lauri tried not to laugh at his solemn tone. He seemed more like a worried old man than a little boy. She had seen Martin and Angie intent on their play, often noisy and sometimes quarreling, but never with such serious expressions. Maybe being an only child had made Jamey less playful. Or maybe he was just a different kind of kid.

He and Lauri walked out of the room together, and she paused at the playground to say good-bye to Karen and her siblings.

"We're going home, too," Karen said.

"Can we get an ice cream, first, ple—ease?" Angie asked, tugging on her sister's arm. "Who's that?"

"Don't be nosy. And no ice cream, I don't have enough money," Karen told her. To Lauri, she added, "If you have any trouble, call me."

"Thanks." Lauri glanced at the silent little boy who waited so patiently by her side. "I think it will be okay."

She left Karen calling to her brother, and she and Jamey headed for the crosswalk.

"Want to hold my hand across the street?" she asked cautiously.

He put one hand into hers, and again, his fingers were so small and thin. Lauri swallowed, hoping she would do this right. And did this kid ever smile?

They walked several blocks to a large apartment building. Traffic hummed along on the busy street beside them, but Jamey showed no inclination to run or jump, walking sedately beside her, his hand still tucked into her palm. This might be the world's easiest baby-sitting job, Lauri thought. Then again, it was early days. He couldn't be this good all the time.

A delivery truck lumbered past them on the street. The air was warm and smelled slightly of smog; a dog barked at them from behind a gate and Jamey shivered.

"It's okay," Lauri said quickly. "He can't get out of

the fence. Is this your apartment building?''

She glanced at the note of instructions her mother had given her to double-check the address, but Jamey was already climbing the steps to the front entrance.

Inside, Jamey led the way to the right apartment, fishing his house key out from beneath his tee shirt. He wore it on a cord around his neck. Harder for a little kid to lose that way than in a pocket, Lauri guessed.

Lauri unlocked the door and led the way inside. The air seemed stale, and the apartment itself was spacious but empty of life and curiously lacking in any real personality. The couches were leather, the TV large, and the kitchen had empty countertops. Of course, Uncle Jack and his son hadn't been back here long, she reminded herself. And maybe single fathers didn't collect the kind of cheerful clutter that marked her own house, or Karen's.

She tried to think what a good sitter would do. ''Would you like a snack?'' she asked Jamey.

He thought about it. ''Some juice?''

''Sure,'' Lauri told him. ''At least, let me check the fridge.''

She found a bottle of apple juice and poured the little boy a glass, then checked the kitchen cabinets till she found some graham crackers. There wasn't much food in the kitchen, but then again, her uncle might not do much cooking. He made plenty of money in his insurance job—they probably ordered out a lot.

''What's your favorite dinner?'' she asked her little cousin as he munched on a cracker.

He considered; he was a funny little kid, she thought, never answering quickly.

"Pizza," he said at last, confirming her hunch about their dining patterns.

"Me too," she told him, grinning. "Do you have any homework to do?"

He shook his head. Maybe first grade was too soon for homework, Lauri thought. She had a ton, herself. So, what was she supposed to do now? Did she have to play games with him, or was he allowed to watch TV while she read her history chapter? Her mom hadn't given her any instructions about what to do after they reached the apartment, except the usual about not letting Jamey use the stove or handle sharp knives, and Lauri would have figured that out herself.

Jamey drank the last of his juice, stood up, and put the empty glass into the dishwasher, without even being told. This kid was a paragon, Lauri thought. He went back to his backpack, which he had dropped on the floor, and drew out a crumpled sheet of paper.

"What's that?"

He brought it to show her. "Ball games at the park," he said, his tone wistful. "Teacher gave it to us."

Lauri brightened. The park—what a good idea. Jamey could play with other kids, and she could sit on a bench and do some of her homework. Surely that was reasonable sitter behavior. She looked at the flyer more closely.

"They have park ball teams for three age groups, including T-ball, that's you. It's sign up time this week, it says. Would you like to play ball at the park?"

Jamey nodded, his dark eyes bright.

"Fine, we'll go up right now and sign you up. Put your backpack in your room."

Looking more animated than Lauri had so far witnessed, Jamey hurried to put up his stuff, while she wiped cracker crumbs off the table and picked up her own pack. She locked the door carefully behind them and they headed for the neighborhood park.

When they reached the park entrance, she saw that a cement block gym sat in the center of the area, with ball fields and basketball courts and tennis courts on three sides, and a big playground with swings and slides on the fourth corner. A sign directed them inside the gym, and Lauri found a line of parents and small kids waiting to sign up for the teams. Fidgeting, Jamey waited beside her till they reached the front of the line, where Lauri wrote his name and address on the form.

A teenaged girl in shorts and tee shirt, who looked not much older than Lauri, looked over the sheet. "Okay, um, Jamey. Go over to the side of the gym; we'll be dividing up teams shortly."

Lauri followed Jamey, who pounded across the hardwood floor of the gym, then stopped short, gazing shyly at the gang of kids already chattering to each other.

"I don't know anybody," he whispered, reaching for Lauri's hand.

Lauri felt downright maternal. "It's okay, you'll know them soon," she said. "And playing ball will be fun."

Jamey stayed beside her until two teens walked out, each with a bag of balls and bats in hand. One was the girl from the table, the other was a tall teenaged boy who looked vaguely familiar. Surely Lauri had seen him around the high school? He had thick brown hair and laughing dark eyes—and she suddenly wished she had brushed her hair before they'd come and put on fresh lipstick.

"Listen up, kids. So far, we have enough first graders to make two teams." The blonde girl read aloud a list of names, and Lauri was secretly pleased when Jamey ended up on the team with the male coach.

He led them outside to one of the sandy ball diamonds, and Lauri drifted along after them. She found a nearby bench and sat down, pulling her textbook out of her backpack, but listening to the tall teen despite herself as he made friends with the kids.

"We'll probably get more kids signed up in the next two days," he was telling them. "But we're going to go ahead and start practice. We'll practice on Tuesday and Thursday from four to five, and play our games against the other park teams on Friday. My name is Mac, and I'll be your coach this season. Who's played T-ball before?"

Several hands went up. "Good," Mac told them.

Lauri, glancing up from her textbook, saw that Jamey wasn't the only player who looked concerned.

"It's okay, you'll catch on fast," Mac assured the rest of the team. He looked up and caught Lauri's gaze and grinned briefly, straight at her. "You'll make your mom and dad, or your sister, proud."

Flushing a little, Lauri dropped her gaze back to her history book. But a grin tugged at the corners of her mouth. Mac had wonderful deep brown eyes, and she thought she'd detected a spark of interest when he looked her way. Baby-sitting Jamey might not be such a bad job, after all!

CHAPTER THREE

With some effort, Lauri pulled her thoughts away from the good-looking coach back to the history text in her lap. But who cared about the destruction of Rome when Mac was so close, bending over the tiny players or tossing a ball with casual grace?

She read the assigned chapter, glancing up often to see how ball practice was going. One after the other, the little kids lined up to swing at the ball perched on the plastic tee frame. The players were inexperienced and uncoordinated, and the big plastic ball often escaped the bat's swing completely. Lauri tried not to giggle as one little girl, her tongue visible between her teeth, swung and swung till she finally knocked the ball about two feet.

"Good!" the coach said cheerfully.

Jamey had his turn and knocked the ball at least three feet. He beamed, and Lauri waved at him when he looked her way. "Way to go," she called.

Next, the kids practiced throwing the lightweight balls

to each other. There were a lot of balls dropped, and little kids ran here and there collecting the white balls. Once, Lauri had to pull up her feet to avoid a ball rolling past, and the two pint-sized players in pursuit.

"Sorry," someone said, and she looked around to find the coach coming behind them. "This is sort of a dangerous place to sit."

Lauri laughed. "I'll take my chances," she told him. "You're the brave one." She glanced toward the group of kids chasing balls and arguing over bats.

He grinned. "They're not so bad," breaking off to yell over his shoulder, "Thomias, try again. Lynn, wait your turn; don't push." To Lauri, he added, "It's only three days a week, after school, so I don't get tired of them. Haven't I seen you at 'Rissa High? You're not in my chemistry class, are you?"

Lauri lifted her brows at the familiar nickname. "Yes, I go to Santa Clarissa High, but I don't have chemistry. I'm a sophomore."

"Ah, I'm a junior," he said easily. "Mac Emerson. Actually, I knew you weren't in my chem class; that's just what us guys call a smooth opening."

His tone was wry, and his brown eyes laughed at her. Lauri couldn't hold back a giggle. "Okay, not bad," she agreed. "I'm Lauri Whitley."

"Your little brother?" The tall teenager nodded toward Jamey.

Lauri shook her head. "My cousin. I'm just baby-sitting."

"I'm glad," he told her, grinning. "Uh-oh, I have to get back to work before someone gets beaned with a plastic bat." He turned back toward the team. "Talk to you later, I hope."

"Sure."

Lauri watched as he hurried back to take control of the pack of peewee ball players, and the practice continued smoothly. She finished her chapter and then watched as Mac gave the little kids a pep talk and then dismissed them.

"Think about a team name," he told the players in parting. "We'll vote on Thursday."

He looked toward Lauri, but the other teenaged coach called from the gym doorway, "Mac, can you help me file the application forms?"

"Sure." Mac picked up his canvas bag of equipment and threw it over his shoulder. "See you," he said to Lauri, who waved back.

Park ball had its advantages, she thought on the way back to Jamey's apartment. Jamey walked obediently beside her, but he chattered away about the practice. "Mac says I hit the ball really good," he told her. "Thomias was better, but Mac says I'll get better with practice. Anyhow, I hit more balls than Susan."

"Mac says" opened every other sentence with Jamey, but Lauri didn't mind. She thought of Mac's brown eyes and wide grin, and smiled herself at the thought of seeing him again on Thursday.

Back at the apartment, Jamey produced a game of Chutes and Ladders from the stack of toys in his room, and they played until Uncle Jack unlocked the front door shortly after six o'clock. He had a briefcase in one hand and a tall paper bag in the other; savory odors drifted from the sack.

"Hi, Dad." Jamey looked up from the board game.

"Hi, Sport," his father said to him, putting the sack

on the table. "Hi, Lauri. I'm glad you could help me out. I hope Jamey was good?"

Jamey's brief smile faded, and he looked anxious again.

"Oh, he was perfect," Lauri said quickly. "We went to the park."

"I got to play T-ball, Dad," Jamey added, ducking his head slightly as his father reached to ruffle his son's sandy hair.

"Good." Uncle Jack told him. "Go wash up now. Want some chow mein, Lauri?" He walked across to the kitchen cabinets and poured himself a short glass of whiskey from a bottle inside.

Lauri smelled the deep aroma of the liquor as it blended with the smells of Chinese sauces coming from the takeout. "No, thank you," she said. "Mom may have made dinner. I'll see you tomorrow, Jamey," she called.

"Bye," Jamey said, his eyes on the cartons of Chinese food.

Lauri walked home, her stomach growling, and wondered if her mother would be too tired to cook. When she reached her own street, she hurried up the walkway till she could let herself in. There were no good smells drifting from the kitchen. She found her mother on the sofa, her stockinged feet up on the coffee table, a rum and coke in her hand. Its pungent aroma was the only scent Lauri could detect.

Lauri felt a moment of disappointment. "Hard day?" she asked. Her mom was a receptionist at a clinic run by a group of doctors.

"Oh, not bad, except for this one woman who yelled at me because I wouldn't put her through to Dr. Humeby.

He wasn't even there, for heaven's sake, he had to go over to the hospital on an emergency, but she didn't believe me when I told her." Her mother took a deep gulp from the glass, then set it down. "You've got to go to college and get a better job than mine," she told her daughter.

And how are we going to pay for that? Lauri wondered briefly, but she didn't voice her thought aloud. "We're okay now, aren't we?" she asked her mother. "About the money, I mean."

"I hope so." Her mother shrugged. "What Uncle Jack is giving me will help a lot. Speaking of that, how did it go with Jamey?"

"No problem," Lauri told her. "He's the perfect little kid, at least so far."

"Good," her mom said. "I knew this would work out. Are you hungry?"

"Starved," Lauri said. "Could we order Chinese?"

"I don't have that much money left," her mother said, sighing. "Give me a sec, and I could make us some fried rice, though."

"Sounds good," Lauri told her. "I'm going to finish my homework." Picking up a banana from the bowl of fruit on the counter, she headed for her room. She pulled another textbook from her backpack, but it was hard to think of algebra right now. Instead, she picked up the phone and dialed Karen's number.

"Hello?" Karen's familiar voice answered right away.

"It's me."

"How did it go, the baby-sitting, I mean?"

"Fine. Jamey's no trouble at all."

"Give him time," Karen predicted darkly.

Lauri giggled. "Maybe. Anyhow, I took him to the park and I met this incredible guy—" In the background, Lauri heard Mrs. Karenski's voice, calling, "Karen . . ."

"Oh, I have to go eat. Call you back later," Karen told her. "And hold that thought—I want to hear all!"

Grinning, Lauri hung up the phone and lay back on her faded blue bedspread. She looked around her room with a warm feeling of contentment. This was home, this bedroom, this house. With her baby-sitting money to add to her mom's salary, maybe it was all going to work out after all, and now she had met Mac. . . .

On Wednesday it rained, a sudden torrential downpour that filled the streets and overflowed the gutters. Lauri wore a slicker to school over her long-sleeved cotton sweater and jeans. At three o'clock she tilted her umbrella against the driving rain when she sloshed her way to the elementary school to pick up Jamey.

She found him peering uncertainly at the steady drone of rain that beat upon the classroom window.

"Did you wear a raincoat?" Lauri asked the little boy as he pulled on his backpack.

Jamey shook his head, looking immediately guilty.

"It's okay," Lauri assured him. "Here, you can get under my umbrella. We'll walk together, like little ducks."

That made him giggle. "But ducks walk in a line; I saw it in a book," he objected.

"Okay, we walk side by side, like penguins."

They argued cheerfully about how penguins would walk on the way back to his apartment. Lauri tilted the umbrella to protect him, even thought she took the brunt of the cold rain as a result.

Inside, Lauri pulled off her slicker and ran her fingers through her rapidly frizzing hair. She sent Jamey to change his damp clothes and looked into the pantry to see if there was any cocoa mix. She had to settle for juice and crackers again, and she put Jamey out a snack, which he wolfed down quickly.

Then Jamey sprawled on the floor with a platoon of plastic spacemen, and Lauri sat on the couch working on a page of algebra. Her thoughts kept returning to Mac. She had hoped for a glimpse of the upperclassman at school today, but no luck. Was he thinking about her?

Jamey seemed to be thinking of his coach, too, or at least, about the ball team. He looked wistfully at the rain still beating on the windowpanes. "Do you think we'll have ball practice tomorrow?"

Lauri glanced out the rain-splattered glass. "I hope so; maybe the rain will stop before tomorrow afternoon."

"I hope so, too," Jamey agreed. He went back to his spacemen, and Lauri pulled her attention back to the math. When it was done, she worked on a sheet from her psych class, plotting left-handed/right-handedness through a family tree, as well as eye and hair color. This was hard. Lauri's family wasn't particularly close-knit, and she didn't see her cousins or grandmother very often. She'd have to ask her mom for help with this.

Then she heard a sharp whack and looked up quickly as Jamey hurled a plastic figure into the wall.

"Take that," he muttered under his breath. "You're a bad, bad boy!" He threw another space warrior so hard that Lauri heard a crack in the plastic, and then—to her astonishment—he jumped up and kicked the cracked figure again and again.

"Jamey!" Lauri blurted, astonished at this sudden aggression. "What are you doing? You're going to break your spacemen."

"I don't care; they were bad!" Jamey's voice had risen. He stomped on the molded figure one more time, and its plastic arm broke into pieces.

Dropping her paper, Lauri jumped up from the couch. She'd never seen Jamey act like this—was this how little boys played? The sudden change was very disturbing. "Hey, stop." She grabbed his arm, and Jamey winced.

Lauri let go at once. "Did I hurt you? I didn't mean to."

"It's okay," he muttered, not meeting her eyes.

Lauri swallowed. She was doing everything wrong. Maybe she had spent too much time on her homework, and Jamey just wanted some attention. "Tell you what, let's play something else, you and me, if you don't want to play with the spacemen anymore. What about a board game?"

Jamey's drooping lips curled into a tentative smile. He agreed to pick up the damaged toy and, with Lauri's help, collected the rest of his figures. They took the space crew back to his room and dropped them into Jamey's toy box, then looked over the toys and games in his closet. Jamey selected a barrel of blocks, and they went back to the living room, sitting on the carpet and taking turns at building a shaky tower that periodically fell down, making Jamey giggle.

His moment of aggression seemed to have passed; maybe she was right and he just needed more attention, Lauri told herself. She'd have to spend more time playing with him. And maybe tomorrow—she glanced at the still rainy landscape outside the window—maybe he'd get to run off his excess energy in the park. And she would get to see Mac again. Had she imagined the interest she thought she'd seen in his eyes? Maybe tomorrow would show her the answer.

Smiling at her secret thought, she picked up a block and encouraged Jamey to build the tower a little higher.

CHAPTER FOUR

By Thursday the rain had stopped, though puddles still spotted the sidewalk.

"Do you think we can have ball practice?" Jamey asked as soon as he saw her after school.

She helped him slip into his windbreaker. "I hope so. We'll walk to the park and see, anyhow."

"Oh, good," the little boy said. He picked up his backpack and hurried along beside her, diverting his steps only long enough to splash through a particularly big puddle at the base of the school steps.

"Jamey, stop that," Lauri called, jumping back from the splatter of dirty water. "You'll be soaked, and so will I."

Jamey left the tempting puddle behind, and they walked on to the park. To Jamey's relief, and Lauri's secret pleasure, Mac was there, surrounded by small ball players ready to take the field.

"Hi again," he said to her briefly.

"Hi," Lauri answered, suddenly shy, but before she

could think of anything else to say, a small Asian boy tugged on Mac's shirt. "Can I hit the ball first?"

Mac waved to the kids and collected his team. Lauri had hoped for a moment to talk, but she hid her disappointment and followed them outside.

The ball field itself was too muddy to play on, but Mac led the peewee team out to the damp grass and found a spot to practice throwing balls back and forth. Lauri found a bench to sit on, wiping off the beads of moisture with the tail of her sweatshirt, and waited patiently for practice to be over.

The last thing the players did was vote on a team name—"Tigers" won—and one of the waiting parents handed out order forms for a team tee shirt and cap. Lauri took one to give to Uncle Jack.

Jamey ran up and peered at the sheet. "You think Dad will buy me a tee shirt?"

"I don't know why not," Lauri told him. Jamey's expensive tennis shoes, name-brand clothing, and profusion of toys at home suggested that, unlike her mom, Uncle Jack had no money worries. "We'll give him the form."

Jamey seemed satisfied. Mac was still collecting balls and bats and saying good-bye to players. Lauri stared at the form once more, trying to look casual and waiting to see if he would come over to talk to her again, while Jamey ran up and down the damp grass, skidding on wet patches and squealing when he fell into a heap.

When the canvas equipment bag was full, Mac walked across the grass to the bench where she still stared at the sheet of paper.

"I looked for you at school today," he told her. "But

I didn't see you. You must spend most of your time in the east wing.''

"Guilty as charged,'' Lauri said, keeping her voice light with an effort. The more she saw of his dark smiling eyes and easy grin, the more she liked what she saw. "I have English and World History and Intro to Psychology in that wing.''

"You've got Mr. Dugan's psych class? I took that last year—he's a cool teacher.''

Lauri nodded. "I keep waiting to find out if I'm totally crazy and just don't know it.''

Mac laughed. "I doubt that. You look pretty normal to me. Matter of fact, you look just plain pretty.''

Lauri felt her cheeks burn. "Thanks,'' she said, glancing down for a moment. "My mom's a knockout—I just got lucky, the right genes, I guess.''

"Now that's biology, not psychology,'' Mac said, his tone mock-serious. "But I'm glad, whatever science we can blame it on.''

"You sound like an expert,'' Lauri looked back at him, recovering some of her composure.

"In science? I'm not too bad,'' he told her.

"In pretty girls,'' Lauri told him, lifting her brows. "I heard you were going with Morgan Comperry last year. She's gorgeous—Homecoming Princess, Junior Beauty, all that stuff. I bet you made a great-looking couple.'' Karen had come up with that bit of information; the real question was, did Mac still have a steady girlfriend? What was his status now?

Mac shrugged. "Morgan's pretty, all right. But we broke up last summer; she's going out with a college guy now, I hear.''

"Ummm,'' Lauri examined the grass again, scuffing

it lightly with her athletic shoe. "Too bad."

"I thought so for a while; now I'm feeling better about it," he told her. "In fact, I'm glad I took this after-school job. I'll admit, I just thought it would look good on my college applications—working with kids, community service, good deeds, you know."

"I'm glad you did, too," Lauri said. "And I'm glad Jamey wanted to play ball."

"Me, too. 'Course, it's sort of hard to talk with a dozen little kids wandering around. And now you have to take Jamey home, I guess?"

Lauri looked at her watch. "I'd better; his dad will be home, soon."

"So maybe we could find a better place to talk? Like, you could meet me at the game Friday night. Or you could even give me your address and I could pick you up and take you to the game." His eyes laughed at her again, and his well-shaped lips curved into a smile.

Lauri laughed, feeling a rush of pleasure. "Is this, like, a date, in other words?"

"You could say that, but only if you mean to say yes. If you don't, you're supposed to give me a chance to save face," he explained, the grin widening.

Lauri giggled again. "I'm saying yes, so your dignity is secure."

She told him her address and he made a note on a folded sheet and stuck it and the pencil back into his pocket.

"The game starts at six-thirty. Should I pick you up at six?"

"Maybe six-fifteen?" Lauri said. "I'll have to check that Jamey's dad will be home on time."

"Right," Mac said. "I'm looking forward to it."

"Me too." She smiled up at him, admiring his deep brown eyes and the way his dark hair waved so easily, one strand falling over his forehead. Were coaches always this cute? She should have hung around the park a long time ago.

She walked Jamey back to the apartment, listening to his talk about the practice while her thoughts were far away, centered on his good-looking coach instead of on the two balls Jamey had managed to catch. What would she wear? She'd have to discuss it with Karen.

It was ten after six before Uncle Jack came in, and Lauri was anxious to go home. She gave him the order form for the team tee shirt and added, diffidently, "I, uh, have a date tomorrow night. Do you think you'll be home by six?"

"Oh, sure," her uncle said, glancing through a stack of mail he had brought into the apartment with him. "How was the practice, Sport?"

"Great," Jamey said. "You should have seen me catch a ball! I did real good, Mac said so. . . ."

Lauri said good-bye and left them talking about T-ball. She walked home quickly, eager to talk to Karen, who was suitably impressed when she called her with the news.

"A date, already? This guy doesn't fool around. He sounds like a dream; I can't wait to see him. I'll be at the game with Brian," she told Lauri. "I'll look for you."

"What are you going to wear?" Lauri asked. "I haven't had any new clothes in ages, and I don't want to look like a total zero."

"You can borrow my new red sweater," Karen suggested. "I'm wearing the navy one. And you've got those nice black jeans."

"You don't mind?" Lauri thought about the outfit. She always looked good in red. "That would be great."

On Friday, Jamey opened his backpack and proudly produced the order form with a check paper-clipped to it, and when they got to the park, Lauri handed it over to the parent who was collecting for shirts and caps.

Jamey and his teammates plunged eagerly into their first game, and lost by two points.

"You played very well," Lauri told him.

"I wish my dad had been here," Jamey said wistfully. "Will you tell him I did good?"

"I certainly will," Lauri agreed.

When they walked away, Mac was collecting equipment, but he called, "See you in a hour!"

Lauri waved back and smiled, and when they reached the apartment, she watched the clock impatiently. Six o'clock came at last, but no Uncle Jack. What would Mac think if she wasn't home on time?

She was too impatient to play any more games. She and Jamey put the toys away, and she made Jamey a peanut butter sandwich when he complained that he was starving.

"Your dad will likely be here any minute, with dinner," she told the little boy.

"But I'm hungry now," Jamey said. "Please?"

She made the sandwich, hoping her uncle wouldn't be irritated if she allowed Jamey to spoil his appetite for dinner. And where was he? Her own stomach was empty, too, but she was more worried about being late for her first date with Mac. Of course, he knew she had a baby-sitting job, but still—what a way to start out. They barely knew each other, after all.

Her shoulders were tense, and she couldn't stop watching the digital clock on the VCR. 6:19, it said, then, 6:20. Darn it, where was he?

Lauri called her home. Maybe her mom had Uncle Jack's work number, and if he was delayed—but why hadn't he called? And at least her mother could tell Mac that she was still waiting.

But to her chagrin, Lauri heard the phone ring unanswered, until their answering machine clicked in. Where was her mom? Had she gone out with friends from the clinic for a drink before coming home? Sometimes she did that on Friday afternoons.

At last, just before the clock clicked 6:30, she heard her uncle's key in the doorway.

He came in slowly, with no dinner apparent—good thing she had fed Jamey the sandwich, she thought absently.

Lauri grabbed her jacket and backpack. "I'm late," she said. "Got to run. Oh, Jamey caught two fly balls at the game—he played very well."

"Oh, yeah, good," her uncle said. She thought she could smell the strong scent of whiskey on his breath— had he stopped for a drink after work, too? She wanted to tell him just what she thought of him for forgetting his promise to be on time, but then he reached into his jacket and pulled out a slip of paper, handing it to her.

"For the week," her uncle said, his words slightly slurred.

Lauri glanced at the check; it was a handsome sum for the few hours of baby-sitting she had provided, and her mother needed it to hold on to their house. She pushed her anger back—how could she complain about her uncle's timing when they needed his help so much? And he was being very generous.

"Thanks," she said. "Have a good weekend. I'll see you Monday, Jamey."

She ran all the way home, puffing and out of breath by the time she reached her own street. As she neared her lot, she saw a strange tan sedan in the driveway, and then Mac, sitting in the driver's seat. His expression was quizzical, but it brightened when he looked up and saw her. He opened the door and got out.

"Hi, I rang the bell but no one's home. I wondered if you had changed your mind," he said. He sounded a little bit distant.

Lauri was panting; she pressed one hand to her side and tried to catch her breath. So much for looking cool and sophisticated, she thought. "I'm so sorry," she said at last, when she could talk without effort. "My uncle was late. I couldn't leave Jamey."

"No problem," Mac said, his tone more relaxed. "You need to change, or anything?"

The red sweater Karen had lent her was laid out on her bed, with the black jeans that made her legs look shapely. Lauri glanced down at the shapeless sweatshirt she wore, and the blue jeans with the stains from sitting on the grass at the park watching Jamey play.

"If you don't mind waiting—I'll be really quick," she told him.

"Sure."

Lauri put her key into the lock and opened the door, nodding to Mac to follow. "Come on in. There's soda in the fridge if you want one."

"I'm okay," he said.

She hurried back to her bedroom, wishing her mother had been home. It felt a little awkward to be in the house alone with Mac, on their very first date. He wouldn't think—no, he didn't seem the type to take advantage of an empty house with no adults around.

Still, she took her clothes into the bathroom and pulled them on quickly, running a brush through her shoulder-length brown hair and adding lipstick and a touch of eye shadow, trying to look mysterious and alluring, if that look were possible to achieve in five minutes. Then she grabbed a jacket and hurried back to find Mac sitting on the couch.

"I'm ready," she said brightly.

He nodded. Outside, the temperature was falling and she shrugged her arms into her jacket. He opened the passenger door for her, and she slid into the seat, while Mac got behind the wheel and put the key into the ignition.

"I'm sorry about being late," she told him.

"It's okay. We may miss the kickoff, but the way our team is doing this year, we may be happy to miss part of the game," he told her, his eyes crinkling in their usual good humor.

Lauri chuckled, and her tension faded. Wait till Karen saw how cute Mac really was, she told herself. They had the whole evening ahead of them, so what if they'd started late?

Mac backed the car out and turned toward the high school, winking at her as he turned into the street.

Lauri smiled back; life seemed so much brighter now. Her baby-sitting job had been a lucky break, after all.

CHAPTER FIVE

Sure enough, when they reached the high school stadium and Mac parked his small sedan in the parking lot, they could already hear cheers and the blare of the loud-speaker coming over the wall.

"It's second down for the Santa Clarissa Chargers, and eight yards to go," the loud speaker announced.

They hurried up to the gate. Mac showed his student ID and bought two tickets, then they went inside and made their way up the concrete steps to the tiers of wooden benches.

Even though their team had as many losses as victories, the games were still popular with the students, and the benches were crowded with teens and family groups. Lauri looked around for Karen and her date but couldn't locate them. Mac found some empty spaces about ten bleachers up.

"This okay?" he asked.

"Sure," Lauri agreed, sitting down beside him.

The sky was clear, but the nighttime breeze had a bite

to it, and Lauri shivered as the wind blew tendrils of hair into her face.

"Cold?"

She was about to say, "Not much," when Mac put one arm around her shoulders.

Being so close to Mac made her shiver, too, but in a different way. "Thanks," she murmured, glancing up at him.

"You want my coat?"

"No, I'll be fine," she told him. "You're blocking most of the wind."

Sure that her cheeks had turned pink, Lauri looked out toward the field, watching the cheerleaders in their short skirts—weren't they freezing?—as they jumped and yelled at the edge of the turf. Beyond them, the players huddled and then charged forward, running into each other in carefully orchestrated collisions.

"Imagine, they do that for fun," she said, watching the ball soar through the air, and the player leaping for it, before two of the opposing team brought him down.

For a moment, she thought of Jamey's strange outburst with his toys—she could ask Mac if that were normal for a little boy—but then she pushed the thought aside. No more baby-sitting tonight, she told herself firmly. Tonight was for fun, for getting to know Mac better.

"What do you do besides work at the park?" she asked him. "You're a good coach; do you play on any of the teams?"

Mac shook his head. "I used to play varsity baseball, but not anymore; the park job doesn't leave me much extra time," he told her. "I'm working on a special project in chemistry and trying to keep my grades up. I want to study environmental engineering when I go to college, and a scholarship would help a lot.''

He said it easily, without any apparent worries that she would think less of him for not being wealthy.

Lauri relaxed even more. ''You're awfully good with the kids,'' she told him.

He grinned. ''I have two little sisters,'' he explained. ''and the coaching sounds good on my college applications, and it's more fun than bagging groceries or bussing tables. What about you?''

''All I do is baby-sit,'' she told him, her tone rueful. ''But it's not a bad job. Jamey's a good kid.''

''Saving money for a car, or for college?''

She shrugged off the question of the car. ''I don't know what I want to do about college; I haven't thought that far ahead. Just surviving week by week is hard enough right now.''

Immediately, she was sorry she'd said it. She glanced back at the football field, where the ball had changed hands, and the Chargers were trying without much success to block the other team's run toward the goal line.

''Sorry to hear that. Family problems?''

She hesitated, and he said quickly, ''If you don't want to talk about it, it's okay. I shouldn't have asked.''

She looked into his brown eyes. No hidden laughter lurked there this time; his expression was sympathetic, and his tone warm.

''Sort of,'' she said slowly. ''My mom and stepdad divorced a year ago, and we're pretty tight for money. That's why I ended up baby-sitting.''

''I know all about that,'' he told her, squeezing her shoulder a little tighter.

"Are your parents divorced, too?" Lauri asked, somehow surprised.

He shook his head. "No, but my dad was laid off two years ago. It took him a year to find another job, and he doesn't make as much as he did before. And my mom has a part-time job, but she wants to be home after school, if possible; one of my sisters has cerebral palsy."

"Oh, I'm sorry," Lauri said quickly, feeling guilty for having complained about her own situation. At least she and her mom had no health problems, she thought.

"It's not too bad; Kerry goes to school and gets around pretty well," Mac told her. "But there are extra doctor bills, too. I try to earn my own money, and I'll probably end up at one of the state schools. But I'm going to make it," he told her, his tone firmer and his mouth tightening for a moment. "I'm filling out scholarship forms right now, and if I can dig up enough character references—"

"Oh, that should be hard," Lauri teased gently. "You're such a bad guy, I can tell."

He grinned. "Right. And if I can place in the regional science fair again this year, that will look good on the applications."

"I bet," Lauri agreed. "I'm sure you'll make it."

Mac smiled at her, and she felt very close, and not just because she sat inside the circle of his arm. So his life wasn't easy, either, all the time. It made her feel somehow more at ease, as if she could tell him the truth and not worry that he'd look down on her as a result.

Then shouts from the surrounding spectators made them both look back at the field.

"Hold that line," Mac yelled.

But as they watched the struggling row of helmeted,

wide-shouldered ball players, the Chargers failed to hold back the Hornets, who surged forward to a touchdown. The local fans groaned and stamped their feet on the bleachers.

Lauri looked from the field where the teams hurried into position for the extra point kick to the line of fans moving up and down at the railing. She suddenly made out Karen and Brian in the stream of people headed for the concession stand.

"Karen!" she called, waving her hand.

Her friend looked up, grinning when she recognized Lauri. She said something to her date, then turned aside to climb the steps up to the row where they were seated. Brian followed behind her.

"Hi, I looked for you when we got here, but I didn't see you," Karen said.

"We got here late, my fault," Lauri said quickly. "Karen, Brian, this is Mac Emerson."

"Hi." Mac stood up, grinned at Karen, and reached around her to shake hands briefly with Brian.

Brian, a husky sophomore with a blonde crew cut and friendly blue eyes, nodded to Mac. "We were going down to the snack bar. You guys want anything?"

Mac turned back to Lauri. "How about some popcorn and a coke?"

"Sure," she said.

"You go on with Mac, Brian, and I'll wait here with Lauri," Karen told her date.

The two guys started down the steps, and Karen sat down next to Lauri. "Oh, wow, he's a doll," she said.

Lauri laughed. "I think so, too," she agreed. "And he's really nice. I like him a lot."

"I should go to the park more often," Karen said, her

tone teasing. "Too bad Mac wasn't coaching my sister's team!"

"Too late," Lauri shot back. "I saw him first. Anyhow, you have a boyfriend."

A roar from the crowd interrupted, and Lauri looked down to see the Chargers making a valiant attempt at a goal. But she hardly cared who won the football game; her evening would be a success either way, Lauri thought happily.

When the guys returned, their hands full of paper cups and overflowing bags, bringing smells of buttery popcorn, they all sat together and munched and sipped and yelled for the team, which made a surprise comeback in the fourth quarter and kicked a field goal to win the game by three points.

The home crowd roared with approval, but Lauri wasn't even surprised. Tonight, everything just had to go her way. She felt light with happiness—no money worries, for once, just silly jokes and Mac to put his arm easily around her shoulders and hold her hand when they walked away from the stadium.

After the game, the four of them drove to a local pizzeria and shared a extra-large pizza. Then Mac drove her home. It was almost midnight, and Lauri hadn't asked for permission to stay out past her curfew. There was a light on inside; Lauri was glad to see that her mother was back.

On the doorstep, she stopped to say good night. "I really had fun," she told Mac.

"Me too." He took her hand and held it. "Maybe we can do this again, next weekend?"

"I'd like that." She lifted her face and he leaned forward to kiss her lightly on the lips.

Lauri felt a thrill run through her whole body, even though the kiss was brief. When he murmured, "Good night," she squeezed his hand once before she let go, then watched him walk back to the car.

She opened the door and slipped inside, still smiling.

"Lauri?" her mother called from the living room.

"It's me," Lauri confirmed, walking into the room.

Her mother looked up from a late-night talk show where some comedian was drawing loud laughter. "You didn't leave me a note." Her tone was accusing.

"Oh, I forgot. Mac was waiting for me, and I was late because Uncle Jack didn't get home by six like he said," Lauri explained. "But I told you this morning I was going to the football game with Mac."

Her mother nodded. "Yes, but you should leave me a note, anyhow."

"Sorry, I will next time," Lauri promised. She dug into her backpack and found the check Uncle Jack had given her earlier and handed it to her mother.

"Oh, good," her mother said. "This will be a big help. I wish—I wish you could keep it all. Do you need anything this week, besides lunch money?"

"No, you take it," Lauri told her. "I'm okay. Where'd you go after work?"

"Went out with Sandy, that widow who works at the neighboring doctor's office. We got to the theater early enough to get the bargain rate for the movie," her mom said. "Did you have a nice time tonight?"

Lauri nodded. "Great."

"Good," her mother said. "As long as he's a nice boy. I'm glad one of us has some taste in men." For an instant, her tone was edged with bitterness.

Lauri hugged her mother, but she wasn't ready for

any long discussion of her mom's ill-fated love life, and she didn't want her mom's dark mood to destroy her own golden haze of happiness. She didn't feel like this very often; she wanted to enjoy it.

"He is, but it's just the first date, you know. I'm beat; I'm going to bed."

Her mother picked up the remote and clicked off the television. "Me too. Thank heavens tomorrow is Saturday."

Lauri nodded. No baby-sitting, she thought happily. And maybe Mac would call.

The weekend was pleasant and uneventful. Saturday morning they slept late, then her mom made French toast and Lauri helped her clean up the house—the weekly cleaning lady had been another casualty of the budget crunch. Saturday afternoon, Lauri went to the mall with Karen and Karen's mother and sister. Lauri didn't buy anything, but she and Karen drifted through the shops and had fun checking out the new fashions while Karen's mom bought her sister new shoes and Karen picked out a dress for the homecoming dance.

"Maybe Mac will ask you to the dance," Karen said as she stood in front of a mirror, holding a white gown in front of her. A few feet away, Lauri looked at a silver dress hanging on a rack.

Lauri glanced at the price tag and shook her head. "Hush, don't tell the whole mall!"

Karen lowered her voice. "But you know you like him."

"I like him," Lauri agreed. "But don't start making plans yet. I just met him, you know." Still, deep inside, she felt a glow at the thought of walking into a school dance with Mac beside her. Or anywhere else, for that matter.

She saw the gleam in Karen's eye and hurried to distract her friend. "That would look nice on you. But the blue one brings out the color of your eyes."

"You think so?" Karen asked, looking back at the mirror. To Lauri's relief, she seemed to forget about Mac and went back to the serious business of finding the right dress for the dance.

Sunday afternoon, Mac did call, and they talked for an hour, about everything and nothing; college plans and old movies, sports teams and favorite teachers. He told her about his chemistry class, and she told him about her favorite class, Intro to Psychology.

"We did this family tree last week," she told Mac. "You probably did that last year, too. And now we're talking about family patterns of behavior—really interesting."

"I did a study of eye color and genes," Mac told her. "Heredity's a funny thing."

They chatted easily until Lauri had to hang up and help her mom with dinner, but when she said good-bye, she could look forward to seeing Mac at school, and at the park on Tuesday afternoon.

Because of their schedules, she saw Mac only briefly on Monday. They talked for five minutes in the hallway, then had to hurry off in opposite directions. Then when she picked up Jamey at the elementary school after school, the little boy seemed very quiet.

"You okay?" she asked him after they had reached his apartment and let themselves in.

"Uh-huh," he said, not meeting her eyes. But he refused her offer to play a game, turning on the TV instead and sitting down in front of a cartoon show.

So, kids must have off days as well as everyone else, Lauri told herself, wishing she'd had more time with Mac between periods. Too bad they didn't share any classes.

When she'd complained to Karen, her friend just grinned. "That's what you get for falling for an older man. I have two classes with Brian 'cause he's a sophomore, too."

Lauri had punched her lightly on the arm. Grinning now as she remembered the exchange, she pulled a textbook out of her backpack and settled down to do some homework. Today Uncle Jack arrived home promptly at six.

Lauri picked up her books and called good-bye to Jamey. "See you tomorrow," she said.

Jamey just ducked his head, not running to see his father. But then, he seldom did, Lauri remembered as she walked away from the apartment building. What a funny little kid he was.

On Tuesday, Jamey was in a better mood when she met him at the elementary school.

"We go to the park today, right, Lauri?" he asked, skipping along beside her.

"Right," she agreed, happy at the thought of seeing Mac, even though he'd be busy with the peewee players. But they might be able to talk afterward.

The day was fair, and the sunshine warm. Lauri shed her sweater and sat down on a sunny bench as she watched the kids run and play.

One of the parents had brought a big stack of orange tee shirts with the word ''Tigers'' lettered on the front and numbers on the back, with caps to match. The woman handed them out to the players, and Jamey jumped up and down with excitement when he received his.

''Look, look at my shirt,'' he told Lauri. ''I'm a real ball player, number five. And my hat—you like my hat?'' He put it on his head, and it dipped into his face.

Lauri tried not to laugh. ''Here, it's too big. Let me adjust the band for you.'' When the baseball cap sat properly on his head, she nodded.

''It's better. Now for the shirt. Want to take your tee shirt off and put it on, now?''

Several of the other kids had already stripped off shirts or sweaters to put on their new ball shirts. Jamey hesitated. He took the loosely cut shirt and pulled it on over his long-sleeved tee shirt. It hung down to his hips—apparently, the shirts were all the same size, and Jamey was one of the smaller kids.

''That works,'' Lauri agreed, laughing. ''Off you go, Mac's ready for you.''

Jamey ran to join his teammates. He swung at practice balls on the tee frame, caught some balls and missed a bunch of others, and obviously enjoyed the practice. Not till the end of the session did disaster strike.

As Jamey ran to catch a ball tossed by another small player, he tripped over his own feet and went sprawling into the dirt.

''Ouch,'' he said, sitting up and rubbing his elbow. Big tears appeared in his eyes and slipped down to make a visible path through the dust that grimed his face.

Lauri put down her book and ran to see how badly

he was hurt, with Mac striding over from the other direction. They met over the little boy, who was still sitting in the dirt.

"How bad is it?" Lauri asked in alarm.

"Let's see," Mac said, his tone comforting in its calmness. "What hurts, Jamey?"

"Just my arm, and my side," Jamey said, rubbing his elbow and hiccupping a little. Tears still stood in his eyes, but he rubbed valiantly at his face, streaking the dirt on his cheeks even more.

"Can you move your arm okay?"

Jamey nodded.

Mac touched his arm gently, and Jamey winced, but when Mac pushed up his sleeve to examine the small scrape on his elbow, Jamey gazed at it, too, with apparent interest.

"I think we could use a Band-Aid on this," Mac said. "Let's see your side."

Jamey shook his head. "It's okay." But Mac had already reached to pull up both the orange T-ball shirt and the white tee shirt underneath.

Lauri leaned forward, then paused, shocked by what she saw. Several long yellowish bruises showed on Jamey's skinny little torso.

"What's this?"

CHAPTER SIX

Mac pulled up the shirt to peer at Jamey's back.

Jamey jerked away, pulling his shirt down. "It's okay," he said quickly. "It doesn't hurt there."

Mac frowned, but he didn't argue. "Okay. Come back to the gym and wash off that elbow, and I'll get you a Band-Aid."

Lauri followed them inside the building and waited while Mac took Jamey into the boys' bathroom. Then, when Jamey, his face a little cleaner, ran back to join the team, she walked beside Mac back to the field.

"Think he's all right?" she asked.

"The elbow is nothing, but—that bruise didn't come from his fall," Mac told her, his tone low. "It's an old bruise, Lauri. Where did Jamey get such big bruises? He hasn't been in an auto accident, or anything, has he?"

Lauri shook her head. "Not that I know of," she told him. "But Jamey's okay, isn't he?"

Mac met her eyes. "I guess. But I'd like to know what would mark up a little kid like that."

Something in his tone made her flush. "What are you saying? You don't think that I—"

"Of course not," he said quickly. "But somebody put those bruises on him, Lauri. Aren't you wondering where they came from?"

People who beat up little kids—Lauri shook her head in dismay at the concept. She'd seen stuff like that on the news, but it had never happened to anyone she knew. Certainly not in her own family—the idea alone made her cheeks flame with indignation.

"You know how hard he runs and jumps—he probably fell while he was playing, or something. Why are you making such a federal case out of this?" She heard the anger in her voice, but she couldn't help it.

What was wrong with Mac? How could he possibly suggest that such a bruise could be anything but accidental?

"I hope so," Mac said slowly. "But I had to take a first-aid course when I was hired for this job, Lauri. And that's an awfully big mark. . . ."

"You better get back to the team," Lauri told him, not wanting to hear any more. "Or someone one else will get hurt."

She didn't meet his eyes, and when he headed back to the kids, she sat down on the bench again, but this time, she couldn't concentrate on her textbook.

When practice ended, she didn't linger to talk to Mac after all, and as she and Jamey walked back to the apartment, she glanced several times at Jamey, by her side. Was the little boy quieter than usual?

"Does your elbow hurt?" she asked when they were inside. She poured him a glass of juice and looked through the pantry for graham crackers, finding some chocolate chip cookies instead.

Jamey shook his head, taking one of the cookies and biting into it. He didn't lift his head.

"How about your side? Can I take a look—" She reached for his shirt, but Jamey pulled away from her hand.

"No!" he said. Grabbing his cookie, he ran into his bedroom.

She heard the door slam.

Lauri hurried down the hall, then stood outside Jamey's bedroom and stared at the closed door. He was just upset over his tumble at the ball practice, she told herself. Surely that was it.

Could Mac's suggestion possibly, possibly have any substance to it? What had caused the bruises on Jamey's body? Could the damage have been done deliberately, not just the result of a little boy playing too roughly?

It made her feel sick just to consider it. No, that couldn't be true. Who would want to hurt Jamey? No one in her own family would do such a thing.

Lauri walked back to the living room and sat down. She didn't really know her uncle that well; he'd lived out of state for years. How could she say what he was like? She saw him so little when he was around Jamey. After all, when he came home from work, she left. But that didn't mean he wasn't a good father, just because she wasn't around to watch, Lauri argued with herself fiercely. Normal people didn't beat up little kids, especially not their own kid. What kind of monster would do that?

The people in her family were not monsters.

Wrapping her arms around her sides, Lauri paced up

and down the living room, too agitated to settle down
and do homework. And now Jamey wouldn't even talk
to her. Did that prove there was nothing to worry about,
because Jamey wouldn't consider such a charge, or was
it suspicious that Jamey wouldn't discuss it? And what
would an average six-year-old know about child abuse,
anyhow?

Oh, it didn't make any sense. Wishing she could get
these ideas out of her mind—how could Mac have suggested anything so ridiculous?—Lauri picked up a few
papers and magazines and straightened the cluttered
room. She collected a handful of toys and took them
back to Jamey's room, but he still had the door shut.

"Jamey, would you like to play a game?" she asked.
No answer.

Sighing, she put the toys in front of his door and wandered back to the front bathroom, pausing to pick up
some towels that littered the floor. She opened the hamper to put them inside, then stopped. Several small shirts
and jeans were tumbled inside the hamper. Almost
against her will, she reached for the dirty clothes, glancing at them quickly.

One of the pale-colored shirts had dark stains inside
the cotton—brownish stains. Lauri had to take a deep
breath—she felt a little dizzy.

Blood was red, but it turned brown when it dried; this
looked like dried blood. Why was it staining Jamey's
shirt?

Surely there was a logical explanation. She stared at
the shirt, touching the spots. If you washed this in cold
water, it would wash out, she remembered her mother's
advice at laundry time. And no one would know.

But surely there was nothing to hide. She suddenly

wondered what her uncle would think if he walked into the apartment and found her snooping through his family's dirty laundry.

Maybe dirty in more than one sense.

No, it couldn't be true. She was making up plots, seeing things that didn't exist. She pushed the shirt back to the bottom of the laundry hamper and dropped the towel on top.

She hurried back to the living room just as she heard a key in the lock. The door opened, and Lauri sat down quickly and picked up a magazine, hoping her face wasn't red, that she didn't look as guilty as she felt.

How was she going to explain Jamey locked into his room, refusing to speak to her? And could she tell her uncle that someone suspected that Jamey was being abused? No, no way.

"Hi, Lauri," Uncle Jack said.

He looked so normal, so ordinary, in his brown three-piece suit, with his tie loosened, and his briefcase in one hand, that all of her worries suddenly seemed even more ridiculous. He sounded like any other tired business man, not a monster at all.

He walked across to the cabinet and poured himself a drink, adding, "Where's Jamey? Everything okay?"

"He—uh—" Lauri found herself stuttering. "H-he had a slight accident at practice, actually."

"Bad?" Her uncle took a gulp and put down the glass, his tone sharper.

"Oh no, he fell on the ball field and scraped his elbow, that's all," Lauri said quickly. She followed him down the hall and was surprised to see Jamey's bedroom door open. The bathroom door was closed, instead, but it opened as her uncle knocked.

"Hi, Dad," Jamey said.

"I heard you had a fall. How's the elbow?" his dad asked. "Let's take a look."

Jamey pushed up his sleeve and showed his father the small plastic strip. His father bent over it, frowning, looking so much like a normal concerned parent that Lauri felt ridiculous for even considering any other possibility.

"Looks like you'll live," Uncle Jack told his son. "Have fun at practice?"

"Oh, sure," Jamey said. "Wait till you see my new ball shirt and cap!"

Lauri left them talking and went back to collect her things. "I'll see you tomorrow, Jamey," she said before going out the door.

"Uh-huh," Jamey answered. He was showing his dad the new shirt. "I'm number five."

Silly, the whole thing had been silly. Jamey was an active little boy; he had taken a tumble somehow, that was all, she told herself on the way home, trying to forget her worries.

But later that night, the sight of that shirt with its ominous stains came back to her mind.

"Mom," she said to her mother suddenly, "do you think Uncle Jack is a good father?"

"Of course he is," her mother said, looking up from the sitcom playing on the TV. "He stayed, didn't he, while his wife took off after Jamey was born, poor little thing. Jack's been very responsible."

Lauri nodded. "You know why she left? Did Uncle Jack ever talk to you about it?"

"Not really," her mother said, looking back at the

TV screen as the laugh track exploded with a gust of loud guffaws.

"You don't think—" Lauri tried to think of a tactful way to say it, but there wasn't one. "You don't think he would—hurt Jamey, do you?"

Her mother glanced at her sharply. "What are you talking about?"

"I saw a big bruise on Jamey at practice, and—"

"What a thing to say, and about your own uncle, my own brother!" her mother snapped. "Don't be stupid. Of course not. Little boys get bruises all the time; all kids do."

"But—" Lauri thought about the shirt with the stains, but her mother rushed on.

"And after all Uncle Jack has done for us, I think that's a very ungrateful and even slanderous thing to say, Lauri. For heaven's sake, Jack has been wonderful to us. You didn't say anything like that to him, did you?"

"No, but—"

"I should hope not." Her mother took a deep breath and her tone lost some of its edge. "If you said something stupid and made him angry, I mean. . . ."

If he's such a saint, why would he get so angry over real concern for his son? Lauri thought rebelliously. Then again, who would want to be accused of mistreating his child? And they couldn't afford to lose his help. If he found someone else to baby-sit for his son, someone who didn't bring up embarrassing questions, he wouldn't go on helping them with money, paying much more than Lauri would make at any normal after-school job. They might not be able to afford to keep their house. Her mom would be back to worrying every month about covering all their bills and keeping the mortgage paid.

The old fear of losing their home rose up to haunt her, and she could see in her mother's widened eyes that the same thought had come quickly to her mother's mind. They needed Uncle Jack's help.

Anyhow, it was all nothing, Lauri told herself. Her mom said so. . . .

Her mom hadn't seen the shirt.

CHAPTER
SEVEN

On Wednesday Lauri avoided the main hallway after first period, the only time she normally had a chance to say hi to Mac. What if he asked her about Jamey again? She didn't want to argue anymore over the unexplained bruises. Her mother had said it was impossible for Uncle Jack to mistreat his son, and her mother should know her own brother better than anyone, right?

But Lauri didn't want to talk about it. She didn't even want to think about it. She would be happier if she could forget everything, she thought, feeling the weight of worry and depression bearing down on her, leaving her shoulders sagging and her expression, she knew from glancing in the mirror, dour.

"What's the matter with you?" Karen demanded as they went into their Intro to Psych class. "You look about as cheerful as my cat does when she's just back from the vet."

"Nothing," Lauri muttered. This was one thing she didn't want to discuss, even with her best friend. She was glad to sink down into her usual seat and pull out her textbook. This was the year's most interesting class, and she was glad to forget her own problems and listen to Mr. Dugan instead. She and Karen had felt lucky to get into the class; it was wildly popular, and Mr. Dugan taught only half a day—he worked as one of the high school counsellors during the afternoon.

"We've been looking at biological traits and how they are passed down through generations," the instructor began, after glancing quickly over the roll. "We looked at eye color and right- and left-handedness, and now, as counsellors who assist at twelve-step programs will tell you, this type of biological trait is not the only thing that can be passed along through families." Mr. Dugan paused and focused his gaze on a tall boy in the back of the room. "Mr. Mayfield, are you with us?"

Lauri looked over her shoulder to see the other teen flush and push the sports magazine he'd been scanning back into his notebook. "Oh, sure, Mr. Dugan. You were talking about steps—walking—joggers?"

A ripple of laughter ran through the classroom. Lauri giggled and glanced at Karen, across the aisle, who met her eyes and laughed out loud.

"Not exactly," Mr. Dugan continued, his eyes twinkling. "Twelve-step programs are found in Alcoholics Anonymous and other substance-abuse programs. Despite the long argument about nature/nurture—that is, which traits are inborn and which are learned—we talked about that last week, remember—psychologists will tell you that children do learn much of their behavior at their parents' knee."

The instructor paused to glance around the room. "Which means what, uh, Miss Collins?"

"If my old man is a drunk, I will be, too?" the red-head suggested, grinning.

"A possibility, but not predetermined," the teacher said, smiling slightly. "Children of alcoholics may inherit a susceptibility to alcoholic abuse, but they also may choose not to drink at all—they have a choice. We almost always do, you know."

"Mr. Dugan, why would someone want to drink too much?" Karen asked. "If a kid's father was a drunk, wouldn't the kid see how much of a mess his father was?"

"Sometimes," the teacher answered. "But remember, what you grow up with will seem normal to you. You have to have an awareness of the problem before you can begin to change your own behavior, if change is needed. Now, what other patterns of destructive behavior are notorious for being passed down through generations? Who read the chapter last night?"

Lauri hadn't read the assignment; she'd been too upset and anxious over Jamey. She looked down, hoping the teacher wouldn't call on her.

Fortunately, he looked toward the other side of the room. "Mr. Mannix?"

"Alcohol and other substance abuse—oh, you said that."

"So I did. Miss Karensky?"

Karen had raised her hand. "What about the kind of relationships you have with—I mean—the opposite sex."

Someone giggled, and a boy in the back called, "Yes!"

"Yes, certainly. Can you give us an example?" The

teacher walked closer to Karen, whose cheeks had reddened.

Lauri turned to look at her friend, but this time Karen didn't meet her gaze.

"Well, um, if your parents are divorced, are you going to end up divorced?"

Lauri sat up straighter; Karen still didn't glance her way. Did Karen have someone specific in mind? Lauri took a deep breath, feeling her face flush with sudden anger.

"Some studies suggest a higher probability, but that subject merits a longer discussion," the teacher said. "But before we get too far away from the main question, what other patterns of behavior might be passed along through generations? Miss Whitley?"

Lauri blinked, her mind a whirl of confused thoughts. Feeling the teacher's gaze fixed on her, she blurted the one thing she had not meant to say. "Child abuse?"

"Certainly, spousal and child abuses have a lasting effect on the whole family."

"Mr. Dugan!" A girl in the back raised her voice to be heard. "What Karen said—you mean if my mom divorced, that means I'm going to be divorced, too? That's not fair!"

"Now, Miss McKinney, we said that you have control over your own destiny, didn't we," the teacher said, his tone soothing.

"But—"

Lauri slid down in her seat, thankful when the teacher walked to the other end of the room and she could be unobserved. She glanced once at Karen, but her friend was still avoiding her eye.

Usually, the discussion in the class was the most interesting part of her day, but not today. Today, Lauri thought, she didn't really want to hear any of this. What did a bunch of dry old teachers know, anyhow? Her head ached dully, and her stomach felt unsettled. She wanted to go home and lie on her own bed and pull up the covers and forget the rest of the world. Forget best friends who seemed to think they could analyze you just because their parents weren't divorced, forget teachers who knew too much, forget even little Jamey.

Didn't she have her own problems? Who said she had to decide the fate of the universe, for crying out loud?

It wasn't as if anyone would listen to her. When her own mother said the question of abuse was impossible to consider—Lauri shut her eyes as the discussion continued around her and was thankful when the bell finally rang.

She grabbed her books and backpack and walked out of the room, not waiting for Karen. When her friend ran to catch up with her in the hall, dodging a group of chattering girls and two boys carrying an armload of sport equipment, Karen sounded breathless.

"Wait up! What's wrong?"

"Nothing," Lauri said. "I need to hit the rest room before lunch, that's all."

After a quick stop at the girls' lounge, they went into the cafeteria, and Lauri picked up a lunch tray. They didn't discuss the last class while they ate, but even so, Lauri's hamburger tasted like cardboard, and she left most of it on her plate.

"Are you okay?" Karen asked, her tone tentative.

Why, just because my best friend thinks I'm weird? Lauri thought. But all she said was, "I'm not hungry."

She didn't see Mac at lunch, but she never did; the

upperclassmen ate on a different shift. Usually, she wished the schedule were different; today, she was glad.

She and Karen parted in the hall and went on to different classes. Lauri found it hard to focus on the rest of the lessons, but she didn't want the afternoon to end, either. When the last bell rang, she sighed. Now she had to walk down to the elementary school, and the subject of Jamey would be impossible to ignore.

She walked with lagging steps to the school, and when she looked inside Jamey's classroom, found him still at his desk, carefully arranging papers on its top into precise lines.

Several other children were still at their seats, too, and the teacher worked on a bulletin board, stapling sheets of paper to the colored background.

What was this, a mass detention? Lauri walked up to Jamey's desk. "Hi, you ready to go?"

He nodded. "Just had to get my desk fixed for tonight."

"What happens tonight?" Lauri watched as he shrugged into his jacket and backpack. At least Jamey seemed like a normal kid today, not silent and withdrawn as he sometimes was, especially on days when he didn't have T-ball practice.

"Open house," Jamey told her, excitement in his voice. "Are you going to come and see my work? I have a writing sheet on the bulletin board!"

"That's great," Lauri said. She didn't point out that she came to his room every day. "Maybe I will. Is your dad coming to meet the teacher and see all your nice work?"

Jamey nodded. "I think so."

They walked out the doorway of the school, where a

big sign proclaimed, "Open House Tonight, 6:30 to 8:00."

Jamey told her how the students had helped clean the room for the expected visitors. "I got to polish the fish tank," he told her. "Before we filled it up again."

"I'm sure you did a good job," Lauri told him, smiling slightly. "Where did the fish stay in the meantime?"

"In a glass," Jamey explained seriously. "And we were careful not to drink out of it."

"I guess so," Lauri agreed.

When they reached the apartment, Jamey got out his blocks and the time passed without anything to stir up fresh worries. Only once, when he winced when he leaned against a chair leg, did Lauri's anxieties reappear. She wanted to ask Jamey if she could check the bruises on his side, but was afraid he'd get upset and lock himself in his room again. And what would she say to Uncle Jack?

So she didn't bring it up, and they built castles and towers and knocked them down and started over. When her uncle came home, this time Jamey jumped up and waved his open house invitation from the school.

"Are we going to school, Dad, to see my room? I have a paper on the board!"

"Sure, Sport," Uncle Jack said easily. "Just give me a moment to get my breath, okay? We'll stop and get a hamburger on the way."

Lauri said good-bye and walked home quickly. She found her mother just inside the door, standing at the hall table as she glanced through a stack of mail.

"Nothing but bills and catalogues," her mom said. "How was school?"

"Fine," Lauri said, shedding her jacket and dropping

it on the sofa in the living room. "Tonight is open house at Jamey's school; you think we could go over for a few minutes? He wants me to admire all his work."

"I'm awfully tired," her mom said, sighing. "You think we really should?"

"Jamey would like it, and Uncle Jack would, too, probably," Lauri said, trying not to sound too obvious. "All in the family, you know. We don't have to stay long."

Her mother gave her a sharp glance, but Lauri kept her expression bland.

"You're right, that would be a nice thing to do," her mother agreed. "Let me change my shoes—my feet are killing me. I should never have worn heels this high."

It wasn't long till they were back in her mother's compact car, heading for the elementary school. When they parked, Lauri looked around, trying to remember what color car her uncle drove. She hoped Uncle Jack and Jamey hadn't already come and gone. She wanted Jamey to know that she'd come to see his work, that she cared. And she wanted to see her uncle with his son; she saw them together so little, so briefly every day.

When they walked into the classroom, Jamey was not in sight, but Lauri and her mother walked around the room, admiring the bulletin boards of artwork and carefully drawn letters. A's and C's and S's and M's covered the lines, the papers indented with the effort that small fingers had made, clutching fat pencils tightly.

Lauri was happy to see Jamey and his father come into the classroom a few minutes after their own arrival. Jamey didn't seem to see her at first; he followed his father up to the teacher's desk.

"I'm Jack Barron, Jamey's father," her uncle was

saying, shaking hands with the teacher, Mrs. Vaughn, who had short brown hair and wire-rimmed glasses. "How's Jamey doing so far?"

"He's a very sweet little boy," the teacher said.

Jamey watched them both, looking a little anxious, but he seemed to relax when the teacher smiled down at him. "He works very hard at his lessons, and I think he's making good progress," she went on.

"Good," Uncle Jack said. "He's my only one, you know, my pride and joy." He ruffled Jamey's sandy hair, and the little boy grinned, even his eyes—usually slightly tense—shining with delight.

How could anyone look at them and suspect Jamey's dad of mistreatment? Lauri wondered. Stupid, all her worry had been stupid.

Jamey lifted his gaze and saw her. "Lauri! Did you come to see my papers? Look, look." Dragging his dad by the hand, he motioned to Lauri to come, too, as he led them over to his desk.

Laughing, Uncle Jack followed as his son pointed to the papers lined up so carefully on the desktop.

"See, I got a gold star on my M's," Jamey boasted. "And I wrote my own name on top, see?"

"Great work," Lauri told the little boy, who beamed at her.

"Very nice," Lauri's mother agreed, leaning over Lauri's shoulder to see. "Hi, Jack," she said to her brother.

"Hi, Marietta. Nice of you two to come and see the brat's work," Jack answered, his smile still relaxed.

"I have a picture on the board, too," Jamey said. "Come over here."

This time, he took Lauri by the hand and led her

across the room to the bulletin board. Uncle Jack and Lauri's mom walked behind them, chatting easily.

"Very good." Lauri admired the picture, where something with four legs and a jagged forehead sprawled awkwardly across the page. "Is it a blue horse?"

"No, a dragon." Jamey sounded impatient with her lack of perception. "Don't you see the fire coming out of its mouth? It's a blue dragon."

"Of course it is," Lauri agreed. "Things aren't always what they first appear to be."

Wait till she could tell that to Mac, she thought.

CHAPTER EIGHT

Twenty minutes later they had admired all the artwork, the cardboard models in the back of the room, and the fish tank and hamster cage. The adults still chatting, they walked out of the school together.

"Are you coming to Mom's for the family dinner Sunday?" Uncle Jack asked Lauri's mother as they emerged onto the school parking lot.

"Oh, yes, I suppose so," her mom answered, without much enthusiasm in her voice.

Lauri looked up, but she didn't say anything till they had waved good-bye and gotten into their own car. As her mom pulled out of the driveway, Lauri made a face.

"Do we have to go Sunday? Do *I* have to go?" Lauri demanded.

"Of course you do. You haven't seen your grandmother since Easter," her mom reminded her. "She's not getting any younger, you know. And she will enjoy having all the grandchildren there, now that Jack and Jamey are back in California."

Lauri sighed. She had never been close to her grandmother, who would—judging by past experience—be more likely to complain about the children making too much noise than to appear to relish their company. And Aunt Paula's kids were unmitigated brats. Oh, what a great family event to look forward to.

At least, now that her fears were allayed, she could greet Mac on Thursday without a nagging worry spoiling her enjoyment of his company. They chatted after the practice, and made plans to go to the game again on Friday night.

Friday afternoon, Jamey hit and ran and caught one ball without dropping it, and generally enjoyed his T-ball game. After they returned to the apartment, Lauri waited impatiently till her uncle got home, so she could hurry home and change, and maybe not keep Mac waiting this time.

She had just glanced at her watch for the tenth time when she looked back at Jamey, across the board game they were playing, and saw that his expression was bleak.

"What's wrong?" she demanded.

"It's Friday," he said, biting his lip. "I won't get to see you again till Monday."

Surprised and touched, Lauri leaned over the game to give him an impulsive hug. "Actually, you will. I'll be at Gram's on Sunday for dinner when you and your dad come."

"Honest?" Jamey stared at her, his expression earnest. "That's good. You do like me, don't you, Lauri?"

"Of course I like you," Lauri told him, mystified by the question. "Why wouldn't I?"

"Sometimes I'm bad," Jamey said, his voice sinking to a whisper, his eyes wide and tense.

"Everyone does the wrong thing once in a while," Lauri told him. "That doesn't mean you're bad, Jamey."

His expression was still mournful. "I am," he repeated. "My mom left, you know. Maybe she didn't like me. Maybe I was bad then, too."

Lauri felt a wave of sympathy so acute she had to blink back tears. "But you were just a baby!"

He stared at her, and she swallowed and went on. "Babies can't be bad! They wouldn't know how. I don't know why your mom left, but it wasn't because of you, I promise. It wasn't your fault, Jamey."

He glanced down at the game board, and she hurried on, not sure how to convince him. "But I know how you feel, Jamey, I think. My dad left home, too, a long time ago. But I know he didn't leave because of me, though I used to think that when I was younger. . . . We talked about this in my psych class a few weeks ago. Little kids think everything is their fault, even when it's not. When parents divorce, or even when someone dies, they think maybe it's because of something they did."

It was basically because small children saw themselves at the center of the world, they weren't mature enough to have any other perspective, but Lauri didn't know how to explain that, and Jamey probably wasn't old enough to understand it, anyhow. But the pain she saw in his eyes, the haunted expression she sometimes glimpsed on his face—it woke a quiver of response deep inside, from the little girl who'd once cried for her father to come home again.

She held him tight for a moment. He was so small,

his body so slight and so vulnerable. His arms clung around her neck, and he sighed against her shoulder. For a moment, they were both silent, then he pulled back and pointed out matter-of-factly, "You knocked my man off his square."

Lauri straightened the game pieces. "So I did."

She gave him an intense look, but this time, Jamey concentrated on the board. He didn't want to talk anymore. Maybe it was good that he had talked about it at all, though. Poor Jamey. She'd only been baby-sitting two weeks; she had no idea that he missed her on the weekend. Maybe there was a bigger gap in his life than she'd realized, having no mother and a father busy most of the time with work. She thought about the yellowing bruises on his body, so briefly glimpsed, then pushed the memory away. No, no, it had nothing to do with that.

They played until Uncle Jack came home from work, only a few minutes after six, then she said good-bye quickly.

"I'll see you Sunday at Gram's," she told Jamey when she hugged him. "Okay?"

He nodded, but he held her very tight for a moment before she hurried out the door.

This time, she made it home before Mac arrived and had time to change her clothes and touch up her makeup. When the doorbell rang, she ran to answer.

"Hi," she said, smiling at Mac. He looked great, with a navy wool pullover beneath his tan jacket, and tan corduroy slacks. "I'm ready."

He reached for her hand and squeezed it lightly. "You look gorgeous," he told her.

Lauri laughed. She'd combed her wardrobe for the right outfit—she couldn't borrow from Karen forever—

and had decided on a deep green sweater with a navy turtleneck beneath, and slim-fitting navy slacks. They were last year's fashions, but still looked pretty good.

They walked out to Mac's small sedan together, and Lauri slid into the passenger's seat, pulling on her seat belt. As they drove to the stadium, he told her funny stories about his disastrous experiment in chemistry.

"So after the smoke cleared, Mr. Rodriguez looked at me and said, 'You have any more surprises in store for us, Mr. Emerson?' "

Lauri laughed out loud. "Did you really blow up the beaker?"

"I swear. There's still a scorched spot on the lab desk; I'll show you sometime. And then Luis, my lab partner, says to the teacher, 'It's was Mac's idea to change the formula.' "

"Oh, that was helpful," Lauri agreed, still chuckling.

"Yeah, I know. I said, 'Thanks a bunch, *amigo*.' " Mac grinned at the memory. "And now Luis swears that Mr. Rodriguez will never let me near the Bunsen burners again. What about you? Anything interesting in your psych class this week?"

Lauri shook her head. "Nothing that compares to blowing up an experiment," she said lightly. She was glad to see the parking lot ahead of them, and as Mac turned the small car into the lot, added, "If we hurry, I think we'll make the kickoff this time."

Inside the stadium, they located Karen and Brian, and climbed halfway up the rows of bleachers to sit beside them. While below them the cheerleaders jumped and yelled, and the athletes in bulky uniforms smashed into each other on the field, the four of them chatted and laughed and watched the game.

When Lauri shivered and zipped her jacket up, Mac put his arm lightly around her, and she leaned against him, feeling a warmth inside her as well as out.

This time, the Santa Clarissa Chargers were defeated 13 to 6, but Lauri didn't really care. Not until they agreed to meet at a local burger joint after the game to eat burgers and fries did anything happen to mar her happiness.

"I heard you blew up the building this week," Brian said to Mac as both the guys carried loaded trays to a table in the middle of the crowded restaurant.

Mac laughed and sat his tray carefully on the tabletop. "Right."

He handed Lauri her order, and told the story again of the failed experiment. "Didn't really take out the lab, but it caused some excitement."

"I think I'm glad I'm in biology, instead." Brian took a gulp of his cola. "I mean, those dead frogs aren't much fun to cut up—"

"Ugh, not while I'm eating!" Karen protested, pausing with a handful of fries halfway to her mouth.

"—but at least they don't explode in my face," Brian finished, grinning.

"Double yuck." Karen made a face, then nibbled on one of her fries. "I like our psych class better. All we did this week was talk about family patterns of behavior. . . ." She looked up and met Lauri's eyes and suddenly stopped, pushing her chair back and jumping to her feet.

"But who wants to talk about school, anyhow? Come on, Brian, I'll challenge you to a game of Space Video."

"But I haven't finished my hamburger," Brian protested.

"Bring it with you," Karen insisted. In a moment, they headed for the row of video games against the wall of the restaurant.

Mac looked over at Lauri. "What was that all about?"

"Nothing," Lauri said, her tone curt.

He raised his brows, but she refused to meet his gaze. "Finish your hamburger, and we'll go see who wins," she suggested.

"Or maybe I'll challenge you to a game, too," he told her.

Lauri relaxed and nodded. As long as nobody talked about psych class or family abuse. Tonight, all she wanted to do was have fun.

When they said good night to Karen and Brian, Mac drove her home. On the way, he looked over at her and said, "I have to go to the library tomorrow to look up some reference books for a report. You want to come with me?"

Lauri wanted to hear nothing more about schoolwork. "Sorry, on Saturdays I have to help my mom clean house," she told him.

She looked away from him toward the boulevard, where street lights lit the dark pavement and other cars sped by, full of people impossible to see behind tinted window glass, little groups of families all in their small private spaces, alone in the dark. For some reason, she shivered.

When Mac parked the car in her drive, they walked up to the front door. Lauri took out her key, but she paused and looked at Mac. He leaned forward, put his hands lightly on her shoulders and she lifted her face. He moved closer, and his lips were warm and firm against hers. This kiss lasted longer than their first one, and she felt it all the way through, and was sorry when he stepped back.

"Guess I'll see you Monday, then," he said.

She nodded. "I had fun tonight."

She unlocked the door and went inside, finding her mom sitting in front of the TV in the living room.

"Have a nice time?" her mother asked.

"Yes," Lauri said. "But we lost the game." She went on toward her bedroom; for some reason, she just wanted to be alone.

On Saturday she cleaned house and caught up with the schoolwork she'd gotten behind in. Sunday she and her mom drove up into the foothills to her grandmother's house. Her mother had insisted that she put on a skirt and sweater, and Lauri smoothed her skirt as she got out of the car, wishing she could feel more enthusiasm for the visit.

Several cars already lined the short driveway; she recognized Uncle Jack's big Cadillac and her aunt's van with the dent in the fender.

The front door was aslant. Lauri's mom pushed it open wider and called, "We're here," and they walked in. Inside, they found the adults gathered in the living room, which had formal French-styled furniture with heavy brocaded upholstery. Lauri had never felt at ease in that room, but she knew it was the source of much pride for her grandmother.

Her grandmother, a slim delicate-looking woman with carefully groomed graying hair, stood up as they came into the foyer. "Hello, dear," she said, her voice calm as always. "The drinks are on the table, Marietta, and there are soft drinks in the fridge, Lauri."

"How are you, Mom?" Lauri's mother brushed her mother's cheek with a kiss.

Lauri gave her grandmother a dutiful kiss on the cheek, too, barely touching the soft, wrinkled skin, which as usual was heavily powdered and rouged. Then she stepped back and nodded to the rest of the family. "Hi, Uncle Jack," she said. "Aunt Paula."

"Hi, kid," Uncle Jack said, his smile relaxed.

Her aunt, a tall, stout woman who was the mother of three rowdy boys, waved her drink vaguely in Lauri's direction. "How's school?"

"Fine," Lauri said politely. She looked at her mother's family—every one of them was divorced, her mother and aunt several times between them. And the two sisters joked about Jack's numerous girlfriends. Didn't they wonder about that, sometimes? Was Karen right, and did Lauri even have a chance of making a good marriage someday?

"The children are in the sunroom," her grandmother told Lauri as the older woman sat back down onto the brocade sofa.

Lauri sighed. That was one reason she felt little eagerness for family get-togethers. She was the oldest grandchild by a large span, the result of her mother's first impulsive marriage at the age of seventeen. The other siblings had waited longer to have children— "warned by Marietta's bad example," Aunt Paula had said more than once, laughing heartily at her own joke.

Lauri didn't think it was so funny. She didn't care to be regarded as a disastrous mistake.

But the age difference meant that she had little in common with her cousins. Aunt Paula's oldest child was only ten. This was going to be a long afternoon; Lauri knew the pattern. The adults would linger over their cocktails while one of her grandmother's anonymous casseroles baked slowly in the oven. Then they'd eat a stuffy dinner in the formal dining room, where the children were not supposed to interfere with the adult conversation.

When she was younger, she'd always made sure to bring a book to read, ignoring the yelling, squabbling little boys as much as possible. In fact, she had a paperback novel tucked into her jacket pocket right now. At least her mother's family didn't get together very often.

But when she reached the door of the sunroom, she forgot about reading. Aunt Paula's oldest son Cal had Jamey pushed back against the windowpane. Jamey struggled in his grip, but the other boy was taller and heavier. Jamey's eyes were red, and his nose had been running.

"Hey, watch it," Lauri said. She took two quick steps so that she could grab Cal's arm and pull him off Jamey. "What do you think you're doing?"

"He's my captive," Cal explained, looking annoyed at the interference. "I'm the general, and I'm winning the war."

"I have a news flash for you; the war's over," she told him, turning next to Jamey. "You okay?"

He nodded, still watching his cousin warily. "I don't want to play war anymore."

"Fine, you don't have to. Cal, don't push your cousin around again or I'll tell your mother," Lauri warned.

"She won't do anything." Cal looked up at her, his expression defiant.

"Maybe not, but I will," Lauri said, her tone curt. "Go play with your brothers."

Cal's lips drooped. "I can't; they won't play, either. They went outside to dig a hole."

In the flowerbed, probably, Lauri thought, sighing. She refused to play policeman to the whole crew. Didn't she do enough baby-sitting during the week?

"If I were you, I'd think about why no one wants to play with me," she told him.

Cal frowned, but he opened the outer door and wandered outside.

Lauri sat down on one of the rattan chairs with faded floral cushions. Jamey pushed close to her, putting his arms around her neck and hugging her.

Lauri hugged him back, even though she was afraid he was inadvertently wiping his nose on her sweater.

"I'm glad you're here." Jamey's voice was muffled. "I don't like Cal, even if he is my cousin."

"I can see that," Lauri said, grinning a little. "He's a bully."

"He's bigger than me," Jamey said into her neck. "He's ten."

"I know. But one of these days, you'll be ten, too. And you'll get taller; you might even catch up with him, eventually," Lauri pointed out.

"Yeah?" The thought seemed to cheer the little boy. He drew back at last. "Tom and Timmy took my cars."

"Figures. Did you bring anything else to play with?" Lauri knew that her grandmother didn't keep any extra toys around the house.

"I have some crayons in my jacket," he told her.

"Let's draw some pictures, then," she suggested.

"And can I have some more chips?" Jamey looked hopeful. "Cal—"

"Ate them all, don't tell me." Lauri stood up. "You stay here; I'll get some."

"Don't tell Dad I was crying," Jamey blurted as she walked away.

"I won't."

The chips and dip were in the living room on the wide coffee table between the sofa and chairs where the adults were still seated; she had noticed the snacks when she and her mom had first come in. Lauri walked back through the dining room—a linen tablecloth covered the long table, with nine china place settings already set out for dinner—and paused briefly in the archway between the two formal rooms.

"Are the boys getting along?" her aunt asked.

Lauri nodded. *Cal was right,* she thought. *It would do no good at all to tell the truth.* She found a stack of small paper plates, took one, and filled it with chips from the big bowl on the table.

"My boys are so lively," Aunt Paula said to the others, her tone fond.

"As long as they don't break anything this time," Lauri's grandmother murmured. Aunt Paula didn't seem to notice; she took another sip of her drink.

"You should discipline them more," Uncle Jack told his sister as he reached for a handful of chips. "Especially since you don't have a man around. Remember Pop? He understood the adage, 'Spare the rod, spoil the child.' Man, did he tan my hide, many a time. He broke a broomstick over my backside, once. I limped for a week."

Lauri paused, and the plate in her hand shook briefly.

She glanced at her uncle, but he didn't seem to see her look. She straightened and walked toward the wide archway.

"Now, Jack," Marietta said. "Don't exaggerate. It wasn't that bad."

"Sure it was," Jack argued cheerfully. "He believed in discipline, didn't he, Mom? Shoot, I deserved it, too. Remember when I painted the living room wall with shortening? Could I get into trouble!"

"And what's changed?" Aunt Paula pointed out, laughing.

"I'm just saying, it didn't hurt me a bit," Jack told her, gesturing with his cocktail glass. "You better watch out, or those boys will turn your hair gray beneath that hair dye if you don't rein them in at home. Jamey, now, he never causes me any trouble. He knows what would happen. You'd better give your boys some real discipline, too."

Lauri paused just inside the dining room as her uncle's loud voice followed her. A shiver ran through her. Just what did Uncle Jack mean by "real discipline"?

CHAPTER
NINE

The afternoon seemed to drag on until at last the little boys were rounded up and sent to wash their dirty hands. Then they all gathered to eat dinner in the formal dining room. When their plates were filled, the younger children poked at their food. Lauri had been right; the casserole had some kind of meat and several unidentifiable vegetables.

Cal thrust his fork into a greenish mass and muttered beneath his breath. Dropping the food back onto his plate, he frowned and looked around. Lauri could see the movement of his foot as he kicked his nearest brother under the table.

"Ohh!" The younger boy shrieked until his mother shushed him.

"Hush, Timmy."

"Cal kicked me."

"No, I didn't," Cal said, his expression serene as he picked up his fork again and pushed the offending vegetable to the edge of his plate.

Uncle Jack shook his head, and Grandmother ignored the commotion.

Jamey was sitting safely beside Lauri. He had announced, "I want to sit by Lauri," as soon as he'd come into the room. Lauri could tell, by the way he now threw covert glances at his older cousin, that Jamey felt safer next to her; it kept him farther away from Cal.

Lauri took another bite and ate slowly. The casserole was uninspired, but it was easier to eat it than to face her grandmother's raised eyebrows. Uncle Jack said no more about his father; the adults talked about sports and politics instead, and Lauri paid little attention to the conversation.

She looked up at the family portraits on the wall while she chewed on a tough bite of broccoli. There was her grandfather and grandmother, with her mom, who looked about fifteen, and Uncle Jack, and Aunt Paula. Everyone wore Sunday best and posed formally for the shot, and no one looked real. Lauri stared at her grandfather's face. He looked stern, his pale blue eyes hard. Or was she just imagining that because of what she'd heard Uncle Jack say?

She didn't remember her grandfather very well. In her memories, she was very small, and he loomed over her, and she remembered being vaguely frightened of him. He'd had a loud voice and been tall and stocky, like Uncle Jack. How had Jamey turned out to be so small? His mother must have been petite, Lauri thought. And what had happened to her, anyhow? All they had in their family was questions. What were the answers . . . and did she really want to know them?

Lauri sighed and glanced away from the photos to the china cabinet with its porcelain-perfect shepherdesses and lambs, frozen in unearthly serenity, carefully dusted and locked away behind glass doors. Perhaps the family portrait had about as much connection with real life as the china figurines, she thought.

When at last the adults finished and went back to the living room, Lauri helped clear the table, scraping the plates and stacking them on the counter. "The good china does not go into the dishwasher," her grandmother noted, glancing into the kitchen.

Lauri knew the drill. The dishes would sit in the sink and on the counter until her grandmother's household help came on Monday to wash and dry and put them away in the glass-fronted china cabinet.

Eventually, everyone began their good-byes. Lauri said good-bye to everyone and got a hug from Jamey before they left.

On the drive home, she glanced at her mother. "Did Grandfather really beat up on Uncle Jack like that?"

Her mother shot her a quick look, then turned her gaze back to the traffic. "Of course not; Jack just likes to exaggerate to make a good story."

"Did he—Grandfather, I mean—hit you?"

"He spanked us all, sure, but that's just one of those things," her mother said briskly. "He didn't beat us, Lauri. Don't go making a mountain out of a molehill, now."

"I just wondered about Jamey and Uncle Jack—" Lauri began, but her mother interrupted, her tone sharp.

"Lauri, we've been through that already. Don't try to make up problems where none exist. You've been watching too many soaps on TV!"

"I don't watch soap operas," Lauri protested. "But if Uncle Jack was really treated as bad as he says, why wouldn't it be possible that he could do the same to his son?''

"Forget it; I'm not discussing such nonsense. Uncle Jack has been very good to us, and you know it. And he's crazy about Jamey, anyone can tell just by listening to him.'' Her mother's grip on the steering wheel had tightened; her knuckles were white.

Lauri bit back what she wanted to say and stared out at the hazy autumn sunshine instead, as cars and trucks zoomed past them on the freeway. She thought about Uncle Jack at the elementary school open house, telling the teacher that Jamey was his pride and joy. Listening to Uncle Jack was one thing. But talk was cheap.

Still, she'd never seen him hit Jamey, hadn't even heard him really yell at his son. So, how could she—how could anyone—accuse him of abuse? Why couldn't Lauri just forget the whole thing?

She sighed and thought of Jamey hugging her so eagerly, his look of gratitude when she'd pulled Cal away. Maybe she was getting too caught up in this baby-sitter/big cousin stuff. If she could just forget the bruises. . . .

On Monday they talked more about abusive situations in their psych class, but Lauri said little; the class wasn't as much fun anymore, and she wished they would go on to some other topic.

She didn't talk much to Karen at lunch, and it didn't help her feelings of unease when Jamey seemed quiet and withdrawn after school. When Uncle Jack's key sounded in the lock, Jamey looked at Lauri almost plaintively.

"You'll come back tomorrow?" he asked, his voice barely above a whisper.

"Of course I will," Lauri told him. She walked home feeling listless and vaguely angry, but she wasn't sure at whom. Her mother had come home early from work; she had a headache. Lauri made them both some soup, taking her mother a bowl in her bedroom. Then she sat alone in the dining room and ate her soup slowly, thinking about her own childhood.

Her mother had never mistreated her. Well, once, when she was thirteen, Lauri had sworn at her mother in the middle of an argument, and her mother had slapped her. Lauri had been shocked and had burst into tears, and her mother had cried, too, and told her she was sorry and promised never to do it again. And she hadn't.

So did that prove that her grandfather wasn't abusive, after all, or just that her mom had been able to resist hitting her own kid? Lauri shook her head; how did real psychologists ever figure all of this out?

For one thing, she told herself, they studied for years, they didn't depend on one high school class, for heaven's sake. And one thing she knew she didn't want to be was a counsellor. She walked across and flipped on the TV, searching the channels for a sitcom, something, anything, to make her laugh and change the direction of her thoughts.

On Tuesday, she was glad to see Jamey smiling again, ready to go to the park for T-ball practice.

"I'm going to hit the ball today," he told her.

"I'm sure you will," Lauri agreed. They stopped to cross a street, and Lauri took his hand. She waited for the light to change and for the Walk signal to flash, then they started across.

A car came up the other street, turning right on the red light and careening through the intersection.

Gasping, Lauri jumped back, pulling Jamey with her. The little boy cried out in pain as they regained the curb just as the car zoomed past them.

"What an idiot," Lauri fumed. "Are you all right?" She turned to look at Jamey, who was rubbing his shoulder. "I pulled you too hard, I'm sorry. But that car almost hit us. We had to get out of the way."

She was talking too fast, Lauri realized. She was still trembling over their narrow escape.

Jamey looked pale. Was he just frightened, too, or had she injured him?

"Does your shoulder hurt, Jamey? Want me to take a look?"

He shook his head quickly. "No, it's okay. I'm all right," he told her. "Let's hurry up; I'll be late for practice."

"All right," Lauri agreed. She took his hand again. There were two more intersections to cross, and she was extra careful to check for traffic, even when the signal lights told them to cross. They reached the park without any more alarms, and Jamey ran to join his friends.

Today the nearby benches were already filled with parents waiting for practice to end, so Lauri sat down on the grass at the edge of the ball field. She read one of her homework assignments and watched Jamey swing at the plastic ball when his time at bat came.

Was it her imagination or was he wincing when he swung the bat? Had she hurt him after all when she jerked him away from the speeding car? Lauri felt guilt—but what else could she have done?—then a strange relief. Maybe Jamey's bruises had had an innocent explanation, after all. Jamey's arm was probably sore, right now, and she hadn't meant to cause him any pain—just save him from a near-accident.

Once, she called the little boy aside during the practice to ask, "Does your arm hurt? Do you want to go home early?"

"No," Jamey said quickly. "I'm okay." He ran back to his friends and grabbed the bat again, and Lauri told herself not to overreact.

At the end of the practice, when she saw Mac bending over Jamey to speak quietly to him, she stood up quickly and hurried up.

Mac straightened. "Hi, there."

"He's not really hurt," Lauri said quickly. "If that's what you were asking. . . ."

Mac looked at her in surprise. "I was telling him to hold the bat a little higher," he said. "Why would I think he's hurt, Lauri?"

She explained about the near-miss with the car, annoyed to hear herself talking too fast, the words tumbling out, to hear the high-pitched sound of her voice. She sounded guilty even to herself.

Mac nodded slowly. "I'm glad neither one of you was hit," he said. "What a moron. Some people pay no attention to pedestrians at all."

"You said it," she agreed, but she still felt ill at ease. Did he believe her? Every time Mac glanced at her, she wondered what he was thinking. He'd been suspicious about Jamey's bruises; now would he wonder about her? As if she could hurt little Jamey—it made Lauri angry just considering the possibility.

"I didn't do it on purpose," she said suddenly.

Mac raised his brows. "Walk in front of the car? I didn't think so."

"No, I mean, I'm afraid his arm is sore, but I didn't mean to jerk him—I mean—I had to get him out of the way."

"Sure, Lauri," Mac said, tossing the last T-ball back to roll on the grass and bending over to pick up a couple of bats the team members had left lying on the ground. "I know you wouldn't hurt Jamey."

"What do you mean by that?" she demanded, flushing. "Who do you think would?"

"Lauri, I just meant—" Mac stopped and looked at her more closely. "Look, why are you so jumpy? And why are you putting words into my mouth?"

"I'm not, you said that like you thought someone else would hurt him, and I just—"

"I didn't say that." Mac frowned at her, but Lauri couldn't stop herself.

"I'm not an awful person. I care about Jamey. Little kids get hurt all sorts of ways, and it doesn't have to be deliberate!"

"I didn't say anything like that," he told her. "Why do you think I would think such a terrible thing about you? Don't you trust me, Lauri?"

"That works both ways," she said, her tone bitter even to her own ears. "You shouldn't be saying—"

"But I didn't—"

She couldn't seem to stop herself. "Or thinking such awful things. I told you, I'm not a monster. My family are not monsters."

Mac's expression was perplexed. "I don't think they are, Lauri. Maybe the question is, do you think so?"

"What?" Lauri felt as if he'd slapped her, she was

almost as stunned at the day her mother—no, she wouldn't think about that. "How dare you?"

"Lauri, calm down. Let me pick up the equipment and turn it all in. We'll walk back together and talk about this." Mac's tone was low, as if he tried to calm a hysterical child, and that made her even more angry.

"I don't want to wait and I don't want to talk to you."

"Want me to call you at home?"

"Didn't you hear me?" she raised her voice, then realized some of the adults collecting their children were staring at them. With an effort, she said more quietly, her tone still vibrating with a strange anger, "I don't want to talk to you, period. Don't call me at home."

At last Mac sounded angry, too. His face had turned red—the people around them were definitely staring—and a couple of the kids looked up at their coach with expressions of puzzled anxiety. "All right, I got it. You might just shut up, you know, before you get me fired."

Lauri bit her lip, pushing back more angry words with great effort. Something was spilling out inside, and it didn't make sense, even to her, but she couldn't hold in the rush of emotion. All she could do was leave. She looked around for Jamey, who stood a few feet away, his face pale.

"Let's go," she said shortly, and she grabbed her backpack and almost ran off the ball field, not looking behind her until she reached the edge of the park.

She waited there till Jamey caught up with her. She glanced at his face and felt a wave of shame.

"Are you mad at me?" Jamey asked, his voice small. "Did I do something wrong?"

"Of course not," Lauri told him, taking a deep breath and rubbing the tears out of her eyes.

"Are you mad at Mac? I like Mac," the little boy added, his tone plaintive. "Don't be mad, Lauri."

"No—yes—oh, I don't know," Lauri answered. "Let's go back to your apartment and play a game, okay? I'm fine."

To herself, she muttered beneath her breath, "I hardly knew him. Two dates, that's all we had. What do I care if he never calls me again?"

CHAPTER
TEN

It wasn't long until Uncle Jack came in the door, carrying a large pizza box in one hand and his briefcase in the other. Jamey jumped up and ran over to investigate the box, with its savory smells of tomato sauce and spices.

Lauri picked up the game they had been playing, then said good-bye to Jamey as he peeked inside the cardboard lid. She headed for home, but her steps lagged as she walked down the sidewalk.

Part of her wanted to go back to the park and find Mac, tell him she didn't mean what she had said. But the rest of her still seethed with anger and resentment. She didn't have to listen to some idiot who made insinuations about her family, whose suspicions fed her own worries . . . and another part of her mind whispered, *But it's Mac.* So maybe they hadn't dated long, but she had liked him from the first time she'd noticed him in the park. And she had hoped their relationship would grow. . . .

She didn't want to listen to herself. Kicking at a brown leaf on the sidewalk, she hunched her shoulders against the pull of her backpack and walked on.

Her mom was home. The car sat in the driveway, and when Lauri opened the front door, there was a delicious aroma of spaghetti sauce simmering. Lauri looked into the kitchen.

"Feel better?"

"Yes, thank goodness," her mom said. She had shed her workday clothing for sweats, and she stirred a pot, which bubbled and gurgled on the hot burner. "Hungry? How was school?"

"I'm starved; it was okay," Lauri said.

"Why don't you wash your hands and make us a salad while I fix some garlic bread?" her mother suggested.

Lauri put away her jacket and backpack, then washed up and came to help. When they sat down to eat, the spaghetti was savory, and the bread crisp. Her mother didn't cook every night, but when she did, it was a treat.

Lauri ate a big plate of the pasta quickly, feeling as if there were a great emptiness inside her. It had been an awful day, but she refused to think about any of that. Now, she wanted to enjoy sitting calmly with her mother, acting like a family. And the spaghetti was good.

Idly, Lauri wondered how her mom had learned to cook when Gram's cooking was so mediocre. Or maybe that was why; maybe Mom had tried harder as a result. She was about to ask, trying to think of a tactful way to put the question, when her mother spoke.

"We have a new salesman from one of the drug companies; he stopped by today to speak to the doctors at the clinic. He's about my age, divorced, pretty cute. He said we should have coffee together some time.'' Her mom sounded pleased, but Lauri looked at her in dismay.

"You're not going to start again?" she blurted before she thought.

Her mother frowned. "What do you mean? Start what?"

"I don't want another divorce," Lauri said. "No more arguments, no more men who tell you what to do—"

"Lauri, for heaven's sake." Her mother put down her fork. "I'm just talking about a very casual date, not marrying the guy. And anyhow, it might work out better the next time, you know?"

How many times had her mother said that before? Lauri found she had lost her appetite. She pushed her plate back. "I'm done. I'm going to do my homework. If you want me to clear up, I'll do it later."

Her mother blinked, but Lauri didn't wait to hear her mom's answer. She put her plate on the counter and almost ran to her room.

She shut the door behind her and curled up on the bed, pulling one of her pillows in front of her and hugging it as if it were the teddy bear she used to sleep with, long ago.

That was just what she needed, another stepfather. Oh, geez. Lauri shut her eyes and thought of the last marriage her mom had endured, and the one before it. It usually started out okay—her mom would be all smiles, the current husband jovial. They would all go out to eat together, and when she was younger, she remembered trips to Disneyland and outings to the beach, just as if they'd been a real family. But later would come the yelling, the shouts, the quarrels . . . while Lauri locked herself in her room and shivered, putting her fingers in her ears so she didn't have to hear the hateful words the adults flung at each other.

And with one husband—how long ago had that been—she'd been about six, she thought, there had been strange sounds from the bedroom, and her mother's face, the next day, had looked strange and puffy even beneath lots of makeup. Had he hit her mom?

Lauri thought about the discussions in psych class and shivered. She'd been too young to figure all of it out, but now, looking back—why did her mom pick men who yelled, men whose smiles faded into angry looks? And why couldn't she ever get it right?

How did you get to a comfortable place, a place where the marriage might last and everyone was happy? Lauri thought of Karen's family; her dad wasn't "cute," he was balding and his stomach pushed out his shirt a little too far. And her mom was overweight, but still pretty, and she smiled a lot, and people in Karen's family rarely yelled. . . .

Lauri remembered one day when she had gone over to find Karen and her siblings searching through photo albums for some baby pictures for a school project.

Lauri had been amazed to see that the Karenskys had a whole cabinet full of family albums. There was their whole history—from the wedding with Mr. and Mrs. Karensky looking young and skinny and strange, to cooing babies, wailing toddlers, snaggletoothed first graders, and kids of every size in every kind of Sunday best and school program and sports uniform—years and years of family life, all there.

In her own spacious house, there were few photographs. If you changed your husband every few years, Lauri thought bitterly, you couldn't keep too many pictures around. The current spouse would object to reminders of past romances. She knew that her mom had a baby picture of Lauri on her dresser, and on her own bedside table, Lauri had a small photo of her mom and herself at a school concert, taken by a friend's dad. They were both smiling; she liked that picture a lot.

Why couldn't they get it right, her family, her mom? What was wrong with them—and would Lauri have to endure the same punishment? The thought made her stomach turn over, and she felt a wave of nausea that sent her running for the bathroom.

So much for the home-cooked dinner. A few minutes later, Lauri washed her hands and face, feeling weak in the knees. She didn't want even to *think* about spaghetti for a long time.

Her mother knocked on the bathroom door. "Lauri, are you all right?"

Lauri took a deep breath, then opened the door. "I'm okay. Upset stomach, that's all."

Her mother reached to touch her forehead gently. "You don't have a fever?"

Lauri shook her head. "It's nothing."

Her mother's mascara had run, leaving tiny black streaks below her eyes. Her eyelids were red, and the sight made Lauri's stomach quiver again, but there was nothing left in it to lose.

She leaned against her mother and felt her mom's arms tighten around her. For a moment, they clung together. Her mom was all Lauri had; she didn't want to argue with her.

"I'm sorry I've made such a mess of everything," Lauri's mother told her, her voice trembling. "I know it hasn't been easy for you."

"I'm okay," Lauri repeated. "Lots of kids have parents who're divorced."

They looked at each other, then her mom reached for a tissue and blew her nose hard.

"But they probably didn't do it four times," her mother said, her voice plaintive. "When I mess up, I do it good."

Despite herself, Lauri giggled, then her mom laughed, too, and they hugged again.

"Come on," her mom said. "There's an old movie on cable that you like. And I'll make us some hot chocolate."

Lauri swallowed hard as her stomach rolled. "No chocolate, not yet."

But she followed her mother into the living room, and they sat side by side on the couch and watched the television screen. Lauri leaned against her mother's shoulder, as if she were little again. Her mother pulled up the faded old afghan to cover Lauri when she shivered, and gradually, some of the emptiness, the coldness inside her eased.

Lauri slept fitfully that night, and when the alarm went off the next morning, she wanted badly to roll back over and go back to sleep. But missing school would do no good. It wasn't as if she had to see Mac at school; he would be easy to avoid. And if she didn't turn up to baby-sit Jamey after school, the little boy would be disappointed. Uncle Jack could get mad, and they still needed his help; she knew her mom was still barely keeping the mortgage paid.

So Lauri pulled herself out of bed, showered and dressed and managed to eat a little dry toast. She barely made it to school on time and hurried into her first class. But though she sat dutifully in the seat, it was hard to make her mind focus on the classes. Lyric poetry and geometry theorems and world history projects—all flowed past her today like one big confusion of sounds and words.

Even in psych class, she couldn't concentrate on the discussion. Glancing at Karen across the aisle brought back memories of her anger.

Mr. Dugan had been out of class for a couple of days with a bad cold, while they had filled in with a substitute teacher and educational videotapes. But now they were back to a discussion of relationships.

"Is it true that girls fall for someone that reminds them of their father?" one of the girls in the back of the class asked.

Great, Lauri thought. That should help her frame of mind a whole lot. Let's talk about fathers!

"What do you think?" Mr. Dugan, his voice hoarse enough for him to give a good bullfrog imitation, croaked in answer.

Karen raised her hand, and Lauri winced. "It makes sense in one way," Karen said slowly. "If you love your dad, and he's outgoing and laughs a lot, then maybe you'd look for the same kind of guy."

"Take me, I'm funny," one of the boys joked, subsiding as the teacher glanced sternly at him.

"But what if you didn't like your dad very much, does the theory still hold?" Karen went on. "Why would you pick out someone who had unpleasant habits, who drank too much, or ran around with other women, or yelled a lot?''

''Maybe you don't do it on purpose,'' another class-mate suggested.

Lauri slouched lower in her seat and tried to tune it all out. She didn't want to hear this, not today of all days. Every time she saw a couple walking together through the hall, every time she saw a boy and girl hold-ing hands, she thought about Mac. They might have been a couple like that, if the dating had continued. Now, it was over before it had really begun. What must he think of her? She could call him, and say—no, she didn't want to see him. Why even think about it?

The class ended at last, and the students spilled out the door, heading for the lunchroom. Lauri pushed her book back into her backpack and slung the bag over one arm. She didn't feel like eating; maybe she'd just hang out in the girls' lounge—although some teacher would probably come and shoo everyone out, checking for il-licit smokers.

Her head down, she headed for the restroom, and Karen caught up with her at the door.

''You're walking off without me again.''

''Sorry,'' Lauri murmured.

Inside, she waited in line for a stall, then washed her hands and stood in front of the mirror to comb her hair. She didn't see any cigarettes at the moment, but some-one had been smoking recently; a blue haze of smoke hung in the small room, and Lauri wrinkled her nose at the smell.

Beside her, Karen pursed her lip and carefully applied lipstick. ''I heard about a new Polish deli that's supposed to have great sandwiches; we'll have to try it after the football game Friday night.''

She had to tell her best friend sometime. Lauri zipped her purse and put it back into her backpack. ''I'm not going to the game.''

''Why? You and Mac doing something else? But it's our last home game for almost a month.'' Karen flicked mascara onto her long lashes and blinked, checking the result.

''I'm not going out with Mac; we broke up yesterday,'' Lauri said, keeping her voice steady.

''Lauri, you didn't!'' Karen almost dropped her mascara. She grabbed the slender wand before it slipped out of her hand, then turned to stare at her friend, her expression accusing.

''I did.'' Lauri started to turn away, but Karen grabbed her arm.

''Why, Lauri? What did he do? What's wrong with the guy this time?''

He thinks my uncle is abusing his son, Lauri thought. And you think I'm going to tell anyone—even my best friend—that? ''It doesn't matter,'' she muttered.

''Of course it matters! He's the nicest guy you've ever been out with, you said so yourself. And he really liked you.''

''We only had, like, two dates,'' Lauri snapped. She jerked her arm free of her friend's grip. ''Don't make such a big deal of it.''

''But you'll never have a real boyfriend if you don't give anyone a chance. What's wrong—''

''What's wrong with me? Don't you start with the psychobabble!'' Lauri heard her voice grow louder; the other girls in the restroom were staring. ''I've heard enough of that in class. I don't want someone telling me how messed up I am, just because—because—''

Karen flushed, but she met Lauri's gaze firmly. ''Because you might be acting like your mother? Is that what you want to do?''

''I'm not acting like my mom!'' Lauri shouted. ''I won't—I won't put up with men pushing me around, telling me what to do. I won't be treated like that. I won't let them make me miserable. I just won't do it, you hear me?''

She swallowed hard, feeling her face burn. Tears smarted beneath her lids, and she blinked hard to hold them back. ''You don't know anything about it,'' she snapped. ''And don't talk about me in class, either.''

''I just wanted to help. . . .'' Karen started, but her cheeks had flushed, too, and she drew back a little.

As if guy trouble might be catching, Lauri thought, feeling bitter and angry and somehow desolate.

''Don't do me any favors!''

''Believe me, I won't,'' Karen told her, turning her back pointedly and taking her time picking up her purse and her backpack.

It gave Lauri the chance to hurry outside the girls' lounge, her face still red, she knew, and her stomach roiling. She definitely didn't want to go into the lunchroom. And she had no one to sit with, now, anyhow.

Strangely, the tears were gone, though her eyes felt gritty and her throat ached. Boy, was she on a roll. Within two days, she'd lost her best chance for a boyfriend, and now, her best friend would probably never speak to her again.

What could go wrong next?

CHAPTER ELEVEN

When the last bell rang, Lauri walked over to the elementary school, her feet dragging and her eyes downcast. When the sidewalk intersected another walkway, a boy came zooming along on roller blades. She almost collided with him, alerted only by the rumble of his roller blades across the cracks of the concrete squares.

She glanced up at the last moment, then paused and jumped back. He didn't even slow down, curving smoothly around her and continuing down the sidewalk.

"Thanks for nothing," Lauri muttered beneath her breath. But she did look carefully before crossing the street. Glancing at her watch, she quickened her pace until the elementary school came into view.

Jamey was waiting at the doorway to his classroom, and Lauri stifled a flicker of guilt at the anxious expression on his face.

"I thought maybe you weren't coming," he said.

She leaned over to zip up his jacket and then gave him a comforting hug. "You know I always come," she told him.

"I thought maybe you forgot." Jamey glanced up at her from beneath his long, sand-colored lashes.

She tried to make her smile reassuring. "I wouldn't forget you, Jamey," she told him. She took his hand and they walked outside together. The air was cool, and a breeze made Lauri hunch her shoulders inside her own jacket.

"When we get to your apartment, I'll make us some hot chocolate," she told him.

"I don't want to go home. I want to go to the park." Jamey kicked at a pebble on the sidewalk.

"But you don't have practice today," Lauri said. "It's Wednesday, Jamey."

"I don't care; I want to go to the park. I can swing on the swing set," he said stubbornly.

Lauri thought glumly that her day was going to be a bummer all the way through. "Okay, okay," she said. "But if you get cold, we're going home."

She was already chilled. She kept his small hand in hers and tucked her other hand into her jacket pocket. When they reached the park, they walked on till they reached the playground. Lauri sat down on a bench, hoping that she wouldn't see Mac—he didn't work on Wednesdays, as far as she knew—and Jamey ran across to the big swing set and clambered into the plastic seat.

"Come push me, Lauri," he called. "I need you to push me."

She dropped her backpack onto a bench—the playground was not as crowded as usual—and walked across to push him gently.

"Higher!" Jamey called.

For some time, Jamey swung and Lauri pushed. Finally, he tired of that play and jumped off the swing, running over to the slide.

Lauri went back to the bench, though she kept a wary eye on Jamey. He seemed really wired today; maybe it was just as well he had the park equipment on which to work out his unusual surge of energy. She watched him climb the tall ladder, slide down the aluminum slide, and run briskly around and climb the ladder again so that he could slide down again. Within five minutes, he had moved on to the jungle gym.

Lauri pulled a textbook from her backpack. The bench felt icy beneath her legs—her jeans seemed thin against the cold air, and she tried to ignore the chill. Maybe she could get some of her homework done.

She'd read only a page and half into her history chapter when a sudden wail from the playground area made her drop the book and jump to her feet. Was that Jamey? Had he fallen from the monkey bars?

She hurried over to the climbing apparatus and found that it wasn't Jamey crying after all; it was a small boy with olive skin and dark hair in a bowl-cut that touched his brows. But it was—she couldn't believe it—Jamey who had the smaller boy pinned against the metal frame, twisting his arm and pounding him with his other hand.

"Jamey," Lauri called in alarm, "what are you doing? Let him go!"

Her little cousin didn't seem to hear her. She ran up to them and took Jamey by the shoulders, pulling him back. He was stronger than she would have thought, his wiry little arms flailing as he threw wild punches at the other child's body and face.

Lauri put both arms around Jamey and pulled him

bodily off the smaller child. "Stop it! Stop right now, do you hear me?"

With one hand still holding Jamey's shoulder, she looked around to find the smaller child wiping his nose on his sleeve. He had a puffy lip, and he was still swallowing sobs. She glanced around, but no adult came running—where was this child's parents or older sibling? Was he here alone?

"Are you all right?" she asked.

He stared at her, then his dark eyes turned toward Jamey. "He hit me," he told her unnecessarily.

"Yes, I know. I'm sorry. He's sorry, too, aren't you, Jamey?" Lauri prodded.

But her cousin wouldn't meet her eye, wouldn't look back at the other little boy. Jamey kicked at the sand that covered the playground area, sending little spurts flying each time his foot hit the ground.

Lauri sighed. She'd talk to Jamey in a minute. First things first. "Are you hurt anywhere?" she asked the other child. "Where's your mother?"

He sniffed. "At work," he said. "I was just playing, that's all. I didn't do nothin' to him."

"He won't hit you anymore," Lauri promised, her tone grim. "Will you be okay now?"

The little boy nodded, then hurried off to claim a seat on the swings.

Lauri looked back at Jamey. "What was that all about? You know better than to pick on someone smaller than you. Why did you hit him, anyhow?"

He stared down at the sand, still kicking it with a force that startled her, as if he wanted to hit something, anything. His expression was sullen, and his shoulders, beneath her retraining hand, rigid with tension.

"Jamey, talk to me. Why did you hit that little boy? Did he do something to you?"

He shook his head, still not meeting her eyes.

"Why are you angry, Jamey?"

"I don't know," he muttered. "I'm just bad, I guess."

His answer shocked her almost as much as his unusual behavior. "You're not bad, Jamey. But you can't go around hitting other people. Do you understand that?"

He wouldn't look up.

"Jamey, tell me you're not going to hit anyone else," she said, trying to make her tone firm. She relaxed her hold on his shoulder and tried to give him a comforting hug.

Instead of answering, Jamey suddenly broke from her loosened grip. He ran across the grass, toward the busy street.

Alarmed, Lauri pelted after him, fearing for him if he darted into the fast-moving traffic. "Jamey, wait!"

She caught up with him just before he made the sidewalk and grabbed at his arm, pulling him back. He struggled in her grip for a moment, then she saw that he had tears running down his face, leaving lines in the dust that darkened his cheeks, and his chest heaved with silent sobs.

"Jamey, what's wrong? You can tell me. What's the matter? I don't understand." Lauri tried to hold him, kneeling and putting both arms around his shoulders, but he still struggled in her grip.

"You're mad at me, aren't you?" he said at last. She had to lean close to make out the words, which were barely more than a whisper.

"Jamey, I'm not mad, but you can't beat up other kids like that."

"Are you going to leave now, too?" he whispered again.

Lauri felt as if her heart skipped a beat. She touched his forehead gently, trying to make him look up and meet her gaze. "Jamey, I'm not going to leave you. I'm not mad at you, I promise."

"But my mother left," he told her, tears still swimming in his blue eyes, pooling and falling past the lids to streak his face. "It's 'cause I'm bad, I'm bad, Lauri."

"You are not bad." Lauri found her own voice suddenly husky as her throat contracted with sympathy and shared pain. "Oh, Jamey, you're not bad, I promise you. You can't hit other kids, but that doesn't mean that you're a bad person. It was the wrong thing to do, that's all. You just won't do it again, okay?"

At last he laid his head against her shoulder and his body relaxed a little. She held him tightly and he put his arms up around her neck and clung to her as if she were his only refuge.

Lauri held him, muttering wordless reassurances, stroking his hair, feeling an ache of sympathy inside. This was so unlike Jamey—what had caused such violent behavior?

She wanted to ask him what had started the incident— had the other boy somehow provoked him? But how?

Maybe she should let him calm down first, Lauri thought. She looked back at the bench. "I have to get my backpack," she said. "And yours, too; you left it by the swings. Come with me, okay? Then why don't we go back to the apartment and have that hot cocoa? It's cold out here."

"Okay," he said. He sounded very tired.

Lauri felt just as exhausted, wrung out by the emotional drain of the boys' fight, Jamey's strange outburst of violence, and then his tears. They walked together back to collect their belongings, and then headed for the apartment. The walk seemed longer today, and the wind was truly cold.

When she unlocked the door and they went inside, Jamey headed for his bedroom while she poured milk into two mugs and set them inside the microwave. When it beeped, she checked to see if the milk was warm, then sprinkled some of the cocoa mix she'd brought over last week into the liquid. She stirred until the dark powder swirled through the white milk, turning it light brown. She plopped marshmallows into the mugs and set them on the counter, then went to find Jamey.

He was sprawled across his bed, his head cradled in his arm, his eyes closed and his chest rising and falling in a steady rhythm.

Maybe he needed a nap more than the cocoa, Lauri thought. She wouldn't wake him. Maybe he'd been overtired, maybe that was the only reason for his strange behavior at the park. She walked across to pull up the rumpled blanket to cover his arms, and then hesitated. His knit shirt had slipped out of his jeans, and a bit of bare skin showed beneath the fabric.

Holding her breath, she touched it very gently, tugging it up.

For a moment, she saw only smooth pink skin, and Lauri felt some of the tension ebb out from her. She tried to tuck the shirt back in, but as she lifted the fabric a little more, a sudden mottling of the little boy's skin made her pause, and her heartbeat seemed to vibrate through her whole body. There was something—she leaned closer.

She saw angry red marks, with purplish edges and several deep scratches and jagged gashes, barely scabbed over.

Lauri felt cold all the way through, and she couldn't move; she felt as if she were frozen in place. The marks stretched across Jamey's back and down beneath the waistband of his jeans. What had caused these cuts and bruises? This could not have been accidentally inflicted!

Jamey sighed and moved a little. Lauri hastily dropped the edge of his shirt and backed away, afraid he would wake and find her standing over him. Forcing her legs to move, she tiptoed toward the bedroom door and pulled it shut behind her.

Outside, she leaned against the wall and tried to take a breath. Who was hurting Jamey? Who?

The other bedroom door faced her, firmly shut. Had Uncle Jack done this to his son? If not Jamey's father, who else had the chance? It had to be him.

Lauri didn't want it to be Uncle Jack. What would her mom say? How could she ever convince her? If only her mother could see Jamey's bruises for herself. But her mom wouldn't even talk about it, wouldn't listen to Lauri's fears.

Lauri stared at the bedroom door opposite her. Inside was Uncle Jack's bedroom. Was there anything in there that would answer her questions once and for all?

She thought about going inside the room and shivered at the thought. What if Uncle Jack came home—what time was it, anyhow? She glanced at her watch, and the lateness sent her hastily toward the living room.

In the kitchen, the cooling cocoa still trailed wisps of

steam, but Lauri's stomach roiled at the thought of drinking even the bland chocolate milk. She looked away from the mugs and remembered Uncle Jack's talk at her grandmother's house . . . how his father had broken a broom handle across his back. Lauri shivered again, then despite herself, reached for the door of the pantry.

But the broom was there just as usual. She was losing it, Lauri thought wildly. And yet—how could she ignore the marks on Jamey's fair skin? Something had made those awful bruises and cuts—what could have done it?

Lauri looked at her watch again, glanced nervously at the front door, then, her lip between her teeth, walked back down the hall toward the bedrooms. Before she could lose her nerve, she reached for the doorknob of her uncle's room and turned it, pushing the door open.

The bedroom was dim, the shades still drawn, and the bed neatly made, its covers tucked severely beneath the mattress. A picture of Jamey, his hair combed neatly, his expression innocent, sat on top of the bureau. The photo was so unexceptional that Lauri felt a twinge of guilt. Maybe she was on the wrong track, after all. How could Uncle Jack be abusing his son?

Yet there were still the marks on Jamey's small body. Lauri looked around, trying to think what she might be searching for. She glanced back toward the front of the apartment, listening hard for the sound of the key in the lock, but she heard nothing.

She took one step inside the bedroom, then another, all her senses stretched to their limit. The room looked bland and ordinary, almost as if it mocked her. Nothing here, nothing here, it said. But the answer had to be somewhere.

She reached the closet door and put one hand out, pushing it gently open. Inside, the musky masculine smell of her uncle's clothing hit her, and she felt her body stiffen, as if her uncle were actually here. But it was only his jackets and suits and slacks and shirts, all hung neatly on their hangers. A tie rack held multicolored ties and several belts hung in parallel rows. At the bottom of the closet, several pairs of shoes were arranged in orderly lines.

He could have been a marine, Lauri thought, her mind jumping in strange directions. His clothes had an almost military precision about them, without any evidence of stray bits of lint, with no dust on the shoes.

Then, in the corner of the closet, a gleam of metal caught her eye. She leaned closer, trying to make it out against the dimness, and finally recognized a belt, coiled like a snake about to strike.

Lauri took a deep breath. Why was the belt tossed into the bottom of the closet, when everything else was arranged so neatly? She bent to pick it up and bring it out into the dim light—wishing she had the nerve to turn on the ceiling light. It was an ordinary belt, leather, with a brass buckle, something dark staining the shiny brass.

What was it? Lauri backed closer to the hallway and stared down at the belt she clutched so tightly. Could those brownish stains be blood, Jamey's blood? Was this the instrument that had cut and marked Jamey's skin? She felt a rush of nausea, just considering such a scene.

Oh, God, what was she going to do?

A small sound made her freeze, the incriminating belt still in her hands. She had forgotten to listen, to watch. And now—out of the corner of her eye, she saw something move in the doorway.

CHAPTER TWELVE

Lauri whirled.

In the doorway, Jamey stared up at her, his eyes wide. "Are you going to whip me, too?" he asked, his voice just above a whisper.

"Of—of course not," Lauri stammered, jerking in shock. "Jamey, go back to bed. I—"

Another sound made the words die in her throat. Was that the front door opening? Lauri tossed the belt back into the corner of the closet where it had been lying—she didn't have time to see if it coiled into the same shape—maybe her uncle wouldn't remember—and hastily closed the closet door. She hurried out of the master bedroom, her heart beating fast, and pulled the door shut behind her.

She heard the sound of the front door closing, and her uncle called, "Where is everyone? Anybody home?"

She picked up Jamey and hugged him tightly to her. "Don't say anything," she whispered into his soft hair. "It's going to be okay." She put him back on his own feet; his eyes were big, his expression reproachful.

Had she caused more harm than help with her search? Lauri wondered, even as she tried to smooth her own expression into a normal smile. If her uncle knew she'd been snooping in his bedroom—her heart beat fast again, and her stomach felt as if it were tied into knots.

She hurried toward the living room and found her uncle standing at the counter, glancing through a stack of mail.

"Hi, there," he said. "How's my boy?"

"He—he fell asleep," Lauri said, aware that she was speaking too quickly. "I was making some cocoa. . . ." That was innocent enough, she thought, looking down at the mugs on the counter, holding the now-cooling milk.

Jamey climbed into one of the chairs at the breakfast table and Lauri brought him one of the mugs, hoping he wouldn't remark on the not-very-hot chocolate, hoping he wouldn't tell his dad that Lauri had been prying into his closet, his bedroom. She wondered if her face were flushed, and if she looked as guilty as she felt. But she had only done for it Jamey, Lauri tried to tell herself. She wasn't the one who should be feeling ashamed!

Her uncle looked perfectly composed as he pulled open an envelope and glanced through the sheet of paper inside. "How was school, Sport?" he asked now.

"Okay," Jamey said. "And we played on the swings after school."

Jamey took another drink of the cool milk, and didn't seem disposed to offer more information. Lauri tried to relax. She found that she was clutching her mug very tightly. She didn't want to leave Jamey alone with his father, but she usually left as soon as her uncle got home. How could she explain a desire to linger today?

At least she could drink her cocoa. She picked up the mug and took a sip. It wasn't very good; the chocolate had made a skin on top of the milk as the liquid cooled, but she drank it anyhow, grateful that Jamey hadn't complained. He hadn't told on her, either, at least not so far.

Maybe, she thought, her spirits sinking, Jamey was used to keeping secrets.

She could take only so long to drink the mug full of cocoa. When it was empty, she opened the dishwasher and placed the mug inside—the appliance held little inside it except glasses, she noted absently.

"Guess I'd better be going," she told her uncle, a little too brightly. Oh, no, he was going to wonder why she was so nervous. Cool it, she told herself.

Her uncle had finished looking through the mail and poured himself a drink at the counter. "Everything okay?"

"Sure," she said, looking down at her jacket as she pulled up the zipper, not wanting to meet his gaze. "Jamey was very good today," she added firmly, glancing at the little boy and hoping he wouldn't contradict. "*Very* good."

Jamey looked at her, but didn't speak. She walked over to give him a good-bye hug.

"You're coming back tomorrow?" he asked, his voice almost too soft to hear.

She nodded, feeling a lump block the words in her throat. She had to swallow hard. "Of course."

She waved at her uncle, who nodded in response, and then let herself out of the apartment. Standing on the outer steps, she stopped, shivering, and not just at the touch of the cold wind that pushed her hair back and chilled her cheeks.

What was she going to do?

She walked home slowly, wondering if she could persuade her mother to listen. If she told her about the belt, about the new set of bruises on Jamey's skin, surely she would have to believe her, this time.

But she didn't really know that the brownish marks on her uncle's belt were bloodstains. Her mother might tell her again that she'd been watching too many TV shows. This didn't happen in real life, that's what her mom would say, not in families like theirs, normal, middle-class families.

But someone had given Jamey those bruises.

Lauri wished with an almost physical longing for someone to talk to, someone who might advise her. If she hadn't broken up with Mac—no, she could never tell Mac. He'd be sure that it was her uncle, he might tell someone, he might—oh—he might feel the same disgust for Lauri that he would for Jamey's dad. The thought of Mac looking at her with loathing made Lauri feel weak. Even though she hadn't known him for very long, she didn't want Mac to despise her.

Her thoughts returned to her mother. How could she make her mom listen? Lauri thought about it the rest of the way home, and was glad to see her mother's car in the driveway. But when she opened the front door and walked inside, she found her mom in the kitchen, setting a plastic supermarket bag on the counter. Her expression was tense, and her forehead was wrinkled in the familiar lines that marked another headache.

"Put away the groceries, would you, Lauri? I bought some roasted chicken and potato salad at the deli counter, and you can slice a tomato. I'll eat later; I have to lie down a while till my head gets easier.''

"Is anything wrong?" Lauri asked slowly.

"Oh, I got another letter from the bank," her mother said, rubbing her temples.

"But I thought things were better, with the money Uncle Jack is giving us. . . ."

Her mother nodded. "We are doing better, and I'm sure that in a few more months, I can get caught up. But this stupid manager at the bank—don't worry, honey. I'll take care of it. But not right now. Don't turn the TV too loud, okay?" She turned toward her bedroom and didn't wait to see Lauri nod slowly.

So much for a talk with her mother. Lauri put away the groceries and found that she had no appetite. She went up to her own bedroom and closed the door.

For a few minutes she paced up and down on the carpet, feeling ready to scream. What was she going to do?

At last she sat down on her bed, too tense to lie back against her lace-edged pillow shams, and picked up the phone. She dialed the familiar number, and listened to it ring. To her relief, it was Karen who answered.

"Hello?"

"It's me, Lauri," she said quickly, before she could chicken out.

"Oh," Karen said, her voice cold.

"Listen, I'm sorry about what I said. I really am," Lauri rushed on, hoping that Karen would listen. If her best friend, her ex-best friend, turned away, she had no one left.

"Well," Karen said, her voice a little warmer. "If you admit that you were out of line. . . ."

"Oh, Karen," Lauri said. "I'm really, truly sorry. And—and I need a friend."

This time, Karen's voice was charged with concern. "What's wrong? Can you talk? Do you want me to come over?"

Lauri bit her lip, trying to think. She wanted to get away, to get out of her house. "No," she said slowly. "My mom has a headache. I think—do you mind if I come to your house? I won't stay too long."

"Sure," Karen told her. "Come on over."

Lauri hung up the phone and grabbed her jacket. She wrote her mother a note and left it on the counter, then slipped out of the house, closing the door quietly behind her. She almost ran the four blocks until she came to Karen's house. She was panting as she stood on the doorstep, ringing the bell.

Karen answered quickly. "Come on in," she said.

"Hi, Lauri," Karen's sister called from the kitchen, her face streaked with chocolate. "Want a cookie?"

"Oh, good grief," Karen said. "Let's wash your face and hands before you get that on the furniture; Mom would have a cow." She moistened a paper towel and rubbed her sibling's face ruthlessly while Angie squirmed.

Lauri leaned against the counter and watched, her throat aching. It was so normal a scene: the little girl who grimaced at her sister's face-washing was nonetheless so happy, her life untouched by any real fear or pain. That was how every child's life should be, Lauri thought. That was how Jamey's life should be. She blinked hard for a moment, holding back the tears.

"Ouch!" Angie was wailing. "I'll tell Mom."

"Tell her all you want," Karen retorted. "I'll be in

my room with Lauri; you stay out of trouble till Mom gets back from taking Martin to practice.''

Lauri followed her friend down the hall to her small bedroom, where Karen shut the door firmly and plopped down on her bed. "Okay, what's up?" Her tone changed when she met Lauri's gaze. "Uh-oh, it's bad, isn't it?"

Lauri felt the tears come and for a few moments, she couldn't find her voice. Karen sat beside her and hugged her while she sobbed, and at last, Lauri reached wordlessly for a tissue, then blew her nose.

"What is it? Is it Mac? Are you trying to make up?" Karen asked.

Lauri shook her head, trying to find her voice.

"Do you miss him?"

"Yes—no—I mean, it's something else," Lauri's voice was still thick with tears. "It's Jamey. I think my uncle is abusing him, and my mother won't listen. I don't know what to do. . . ."

She told Karen the story of seeing the cuts and bruises on Jamey's body, and then how she had gone into her uncle's bedroom and found the belt with—maybe—bloodstains tossed into the back of the closet.

Karen listened with dawning horror on her face. "Oh, man, that's awful," she said softly. "If that were my brother, my sister—I'd just die, Lauri. Poor little Jamey."

Lauri nodded, and swallowed a sob, trying not to start bawling all over again. "But I don't know what to do," she repeated.

Karen stared at her, frowning. "Lauri, did you say that you picked up the belt?"

"Sure, I told you, I looked at the buckle and—"

"But, Lauri, that means your fingerprints are on the

belt now,'' Karen exclaimed, her eyes big. ''That's how innocent people always get accused on the cop shows. Don't you see? You can't go to the police. What if your uncle tells them that you're the one who beat up Jamey?''

''But I would never—'' Lauri began, horrified at the thought.

''I know that and you know that, but you've been baby-sitting him every day. You had the opportunity. And if they find your fingerprints on the belt . . .''

Lauri swallowed hard. Just by trying to find evidence, she'd made the situation even harder to resolve. She shuddered, thinking of policemen staring at her with unbelieving eyes. Would they put her in jail? And Jamey would be no better off; in fact, he would be bitterly hurt if Lauri stopped coming. Almost every day when she left, he asked her if she was coming back.

By trying to help, she had only made things worse.

She and Karen talked for an hour, but every idea Lauri thought of seemed to lead to a blind alley. ''If I tell the police first, surely they won't think I could be guilty,'' she argued.

''Maybe, maybe not,'' Karen said. ''You know how it goes on those shows on TV.''

When she finally walked home alone, Lauri found her shoulders sagging and her steps slow. She was no closer to any hope of a resolution than she had been. She had to talk to an adult, to someone who might know the best course of action to take. Someone who knew about child abuse, and bad stuff like that.

When she let herself into her house, Lauri found the

front part of the house dark, and her mom still in her bedroom. Her mother probably hadn't even noticed that Lauri had been gone.

She walked down the hall and knocked softly on the bedroom door. "How's your head?" she called.

"A little better," her mother answered, her voice groggy with sleep.

"Want me to bring you something to eat?" Lauri asked.

"No thanks, maybe later," her mother answered. Lauri could hear the bed creak as her mother settled herself beneath the blankets. "Did you eat something?"

"Sure," Lauri lied. She headed back for the kitchen and took out a piece of chicken and a little salad, but found the food hard to swallow. Her stomach was still in knots, and until she had figured out what to do, she could hardly concentrate on anything else. She had homework to do, but when she opened a book, she found that she'd read the same page three times and still had no idea what the words meant.

She pushed the book back into her bag and went to bed. But even that did no good; she lay on her mattress, her body stiff with tension, and stared at the dim shadows in the corners of her room. How could she help Jamey? How could she avoid being accused of something she didn't do? And what would her mother say if Lauri's actions cost them their home? Was there any way out of this mess?

Not that she could see. She tossed and turned for hours and fell into a fitful sleep just minutes, or so it felt, before her alarm buzzed.

Lauri turned off the alarm clock and sat up, weary and sluggish. But today of all days, she couldn't miss

school. Some time in the middle of the long night, she'd
had an idea, and it caused the first flare of hope she'd
had in days.

She quickly showered and dressed and headed for the
high school, arriving several minutes early. It gave her
time to head down to the main hall and find the office
with "Counsellor" printed on the small plate on the
door.

Inside, she saw two inner offices. The doors had glass
panes in the top half, and inside the right-hand office,
she could see Mr. Dugan sitting at his desk, talking to
a teenaged boy.

Lauri hovered outside, not sure what to do. The first
bell would ring soon, and she'd have to go to class. But
she wanted to see Mr. Dugan alone, not in the classroom
where everyone else could overhear their conversation.

The boy sitting at this desk talked in a low voice, and
Lauri couldn't hear what they were saying—didn't want
to hear—just wanted him to leave. But not until the
warning bell buzzed outside in the hall did the boy stand
up to go.

Mr. Dugan walked to the doorway of his office, shook
hands briefly with the boy, and then turned to Lauri.

"Can I do something for you, Ms. Whitley?" he
asked, smiling at her.

"I—I'd like to talk to you, if I could, but I need to
do it after school. Is that possible?"

"I can stay a little bit late, if that would help you,"
Mr. Dugan agreed. "Four o'clock?"

"Yes, thank you!" Lauri told him, then ran for the
hallway and her first class.

She got into her seat just before the final bell, and
sighed in relief. Mr. Dugan would know what to do. At

last, she had someone else who could shoulder this enormous burden. She felt easier already, and could even try to listen to her teacher as the English class got underway.

It was almost a normal day, as much as Lauri could remember what normal was—her life seemed to have been in chaos for much too long—until the middle of the morning, when she walked down the hall and caught a glimpse of Mac, talking to another girl.

The sight stabbed her like a blade. She jerked a little and almost walked into another student, who jumped back just in time.

"Sorry," she muttered to the freshman, who made a face at her and kept going.

Oh, no, now Mac had looked up, and he met her gaze.

For an instant, they stared at each other. Lauri seemed unable to move; she was breathing quickly, and there was so much she wanted to say—but she couldn't, she couldn't speak—because the important things were impossible to say, and neither of them cared about polite excuses.

Mac's expression was hard to read, but his eyes seemed angry and still, and his mouth thin. After a long moment, he looked back down at the girl who'd been chatting with him and smiled. At her. Not at Lauri.

Lauri hurried on down the hall, biting her lip and trying to think of anything, anything other than Mac. It hurt so much to see him with someone else. Well, what had she thought? That two dates would make Lauri his girlfriend, gain his loyalty forever? Just because she had hoped their relationship would grow . . . And now it was over before they'd had a chance to find out if they could care about each other, and Mac had already found someone new. She was cute, petite, with long, blonde hair.

And Mac was so good-looking himself; he'd have no problem getting dates with other girls. He didn't need Lauri.

Maybe Karen was right, and she was never going to have a real boyfriend, a normal relationship. The thought weighed her down, and not until she went into psych class and the sight of Mr. Dugan reminded her of the upcoming meeting, was she able to push the thoughts of Mac to the back of her mind.

Jamey was hurting, would keep on being hurt if Lauri didn't take action. That was more important than her own troubles, her own concerns, even more important than Mac and her regrets about what might have been.

CHAPTER THIRTEEN

When the last bell rang, Lauri hurried to put away her books and was one of the first students to rush through the outer doors. Today she was anxious to walk the few blocks to the elementary school and find Jamey.

When she reached the lower school, she strode through the hallway to Jamey's room and found the children just leaving. Jamey still sat at his desk, putting his tablet away and arranging his pencils inside the desk with his usual careful attention to detail.

"Hi, Lauri," he said, his normally somber expression breaking into a smile.

"Come on, we need to hurry," she told him.

Jamey's smile faded and he looked immediately anxious. "Why?"

"I'll tell you in a minute. Get your backpack and your jacket, and let's go," Lauri said. Jamey got his jacket from one of the hooks on the wall and pulled his bag out from under his desk. She held his jacket so that he could slip his arms into the right holes, and then zipped it for him. Jamie picked up his backpack and they headed for the door.

Jamey followed her without complaint until they reached the corner. When she turned back toward the high school, he stopped and looked up at her.

"Where're we going, Lauri? The park's that way. I have practice; it's Thursday, remember?"

Oh, rats, she'd forgotten about T-ball. And Jamey already looked suspicious; what if he wouldn't even talk to Mr. Dugan? Or wouldn't tell the counsellor the truth? Lauri saw a dozen ways her plan might not work. But it was still the best one she could think of; she had to try.

"Look, Jamie," she said, deciding to postpone the real explanation until she'd at least gotten them to the counsellor's office. "I have to go back to the high school for a minute; we'll get to practice soon."

"But we'll be late! Mac will be mad at me," Jamey argued, his brow creased.

"Mac won't be mad. And we won't be too late; that's why I said 'hurry,' okay?" she told him, hoping the words sounded sincere. *It's for your own good, Jamey,* she thought. *Please, please, don't argue now.*

Jamey looked back at the park, frowning, then reluctantly caught up with Lauri. "You better be fast!" he told her.

They almost ran the rest of the way to the high school, and the whole way, Lauri thought about how on earth she could convince Jamey to talk to Mr. Dugan. If he wouldn't open up to the counsellor, if the little boy wouldn't tell the truth about his injuries, her whole attempt would be useless.

Lauri found her heart beating fast when they climbed

the steps to the high school. The familiar smell of disinfectant, books, and chalk dust met them as they pushed through the double doors, but the school was unusually quiet at this hour. The corridors were almost deserted. A custodian pushed a wide broom, collecting scattered papers that littered the tile floor.

Most of the classrooms were empty. They passed one room where a teacher still sat at her desk, her head down as she worked on a stack of papers in front of her. From the end of the hall, Lauri could hear distant sounds of music as the school band rehearsed. Jamey stared at the bulletin boards covered with bright-colored flyers and announcements and paused to inspect a collection of shiny sports awards sitting inside a glass case. She held his hand tightly inside her own—was her palm sweating?—and tugged him on.

When they reached the counsellor's office, Lauri opened the door and led the little boy inside. Three plastic chairs lined one side of the office, and a rack with college catalogues and application forms filled the other wall. Lauri took a deep breath; her body felt stiff with tension. She still didn't know if Jamey would talk to her teacher. She looked at the inner office—the door was ajar—and saw Mr. Dugan on the phone.

"Sit right here," she told Jamey. "I won't be a sec."

He climbed into one of the chairs, his legs not quite touching the floor, looking very small and vulnerable. The sight made Lauri all the more determined. She had to try; if this worked, maybe they could get help for Jamey. What her mother, her uncle would say—she couldn't think about that right now, or she'd lose her nerve.

She knocked on the inner door, and Mr. Dugan looked

up and waved to her to come inside. Lauri opened the door and stepped in, shutting the door behind her. If she could explain the situation first, maybe Mr. Dugan would know how to get Jamey to open up; it was the counsellor's job, after all. He would know more than she did about talking to little kids.

"Hello, Ms. Whitley. Come in." Mr. Dugan replaced the phone in its receiver and leaned back a little in his chair. He had loosened his tie, and he looked tired.

"Thanks for letting me come," she told him, "and for staying late."

"I'm always here if a student needs to talk," he said. "Now, what can I do for you?" The counsellor smiled slightly at her, and she felt a little of her tension ease.

"It's not really me," she said, "It's—it's about my cousin. He—I saw—There's a—a family problem, and I think . . ." It was harder than she'd thought to tell anyone, even Mr. Dugan, whom she liked a lot. The words seemed to lodge in her throat, and she had to force them out.

"Is your cousin a student at the high school?" Mr. Dugan sat up a little straighter.

She shook her head. "No, I brought him with me. He's only six. He—"

"Ah, do his parents know that he's here?" Mr. Dugan's smile had faded.

"No, I mean—that's the problem. . . ."

The counsellor sighed. "Ms. Whitley, I appreciate your desire to help, but you do realize that I cannot talk to a minor child who is not one of our students, not without the permission of his parents."

Lauri stared at him in dismay. "Not ever?"

"Not without a court order," he said. "I'd be happy to talk to you, however."

Lauri shook her head. She felt her eyes fill with tears and had to bite her lip to keep from crying. She'd lain awake most of the night, just fighting for the resolution it had taken to bring Jamey here, and now Mr. Dugan couldn't help her, couldn't help Jamey.

"Also, I'd be happy to recommend several good family counsellors if your cousin's family needs to work through some difficulties," Mr. Dugan was saying. He pulled the top drawer open and reached inside his desk, taking out a sheet of paper. "Here are some very good people whom I'm sure your relatives would find helpful."

Lauri nodded, taking the sheet of paper. She wasn't sure she could talk, and she blinked, trying not to break down in front of the counsellor.

"I'm sorry I can't do more," Mr. Dugan told her, his voice gentle.

She stood up and backed out of the office. "Thanks anyhow," she said, her voice scratchy.

In the outer office, Jamey squirmed on his chair. "Can we go to the park, now?" he demanded.

"Okay," Lauri said, pushing the paper into her jeans pocket. "Sure."

They walked quickly to the park, Jamey skipping along beside her, chattering about the game. "We're going to win this week, Lauri."

Lauri nodded, but she was too limp with disappointment to care about the results of tomorrow's T-ball game. Her wonderful plan had come to nothing. Maybe she should just give up and accept that there was nothing she could do. Maybe her mother was right, and Karen was right. She should keep her mouth shut. . . .

When they reached the ball field, Jamey ran across to join his teammates, who were already in position on the field. Lauri sat down on a bench a few yards across the park. She could keep an eye on Jamey from here, but she was too far away to hear the children's chatter.

She glanced quickly at Mac, whose tall frame was bent over one of the pint-sized ball players, patiently showing the little girl how to hold the bat, then looked away again. She didn't want Mac to raise his head and see her watching. He might think she was still interested, that she still cared.

Of course she didn't. But even though she looked down at her lap, staring at her hands clasped tightly together, his image remained in her mind and refused to fade. Despite his strength, Mac was always so gentle with the little kids.

From that thought it was only an instant to remembering how it had felt to have his arm around her shoulders, the tingle of excitement she had experienced when he had kissed her. She thought about how it had felt to kiss him, how firm his touch was, and yet how sensitive. If only she could walk up to him now and say something, anything . . . explain how much she wanted to go on seeing him. Yet there was still the question of Jamey.

Lauri sighed and pulled one of her textbooks out of her backpack. She had homework to do; she didn't need to waste her time thinking about a romance that had ended before it had really begun. What made her think that Mac wanted her back, anyhow?

Did he have a new girlfriend already? She thought of the girl she had seen him with at school, the two of them standing so close. The idea of Mac with another girl made her bite her lip. Yet who could blame him?

She felt incredibly alone. Maybe she was going to be just like her mother, never able to maintain a relationship with any decent guy. Lauri blinked hard, and the words on the page in front of her blurred despite her efforts.

She looked up again, quickly, and saw that Jamey was standing in a line of teammates, waiting for his turn to practice hitting the ball. He saw her watching and waved happily, and she lifted her hand in answer.

Mac, standing a few feet away from Jamey, looked at her briefly, then turned away.

Lauri, her hand still in the air, stiffened. She felt her cheeks redden as she dropped her hand at once and stared resolutely down at the textbook. It didn't matter, she told herself fiercely. She had no room in her life for guys right now. She couldn't even cope with Jamey's problems; how could she waste any time worrying about her own incipient love life, or lack of it?

Still, it wasn't fair, she thought. Maybe she'd spend the rest of her life sitting home alone. Then Lauri swallowed hard, ashamed of thinking only of herself. Jamey's problems were much worse than her own, and she'd made no progress in finding him help. How could she possibly think about herself right now?

Besides, she had a geometry test tomorrow, and at this rate, she was going to flunk it. She'd better think about that. Lauri read the page again and tried to focus on the words.

When T-ball practice ended, she put her books into her backpack and waited for Jamey to join her, refusing to walk across the field, where she might have to speak to Mac.

Her cousin took his time, kicking a plastic ball around

the field and chattering with another player, then linger-
ing to watch Mac pick up the scattered equipment.

"Come on," Lauri muttered beneath her breath.
"Stop wasting time, Jamey."

She folded her arms, still refusing to go close enough
so that she'd either have to speak to Mac or give him
an obvious snub. Worse, what if she did speak to him,
and he turned away, just as he had done when he'd seen
her looking toward him? Her cheeks burned at the mere
thought of such a public rejection.

So she turned her back, waiting for Jamey to remember that it was time to go home. Maybe if she started
walking slowly for the park entrance, the little boy
would notice and take the hint.

She walked a few feet away and looked over her
shoulder. Drat the kid! He still chatted with Mac, almost
the only child left on the ball field.

Lauri looked at her watch and finally had to turn back
and yell, "Jamey, come on!"

She watched the little boy as he looked her way. He
waved but didn't break into a trot until Mac said something impossible for her to hear.

Lauri refused to watch the coach; she leaned against
a swing set and stared at the kids on the play equipment,
waiting for Jamey to finally catch up with her.

"Can we swing, Lauri? You could push me," he told
her.

"No, it's late," Lauri said. "We have to get back to
the apartment. Your dad will be home soon, and he'll
wonder where we are."

"Oh," Jamey said. For a few minutes he walked silently beside her, taking her hand when she reached for
his at the park entrance. They waited for the light to

change, and then crossed the wide avenue.

"Mac said I hit the ball real good today," Jamey told her suddenly.

"I know; I saw you," Lauri agreed. "You're a good T-ball player."

The little boy grinned up at her. "We can't be late tomorrow, Lauri. Mac told the team we can't play if we're late, and tomorrow's the game. So we can't be late, okay?" He repeated, his voice too high.

Lauri nodded. "Don't worry; we'll be on time," she promised. Now that she knew there was no help to be had from her teacher, Lauri thought glumly, there was no reason for them to be late.

When they reached the apartment, she unlocked the door, but Jamey hesitated on the threshold. The apartment smelled stale and empty.

"You're coming back tomorrow?" he whispered.

"Of course," Lauri told him.

"And you—

"I won't be late," Lauri interjected.

When her uncle arrived ten minutes later, Lauri said good-bye to Jamey and walked home. She hadn't wanted to look her uncle in the eye, and Jamey always got even quieter than usual when her father was around. Why? Lauri felt as if her backpack held the weight of a mountain. If Jamey was being abused—and she had seen the marks on his body—how was she going to get him help? Could she make a difference, or was it stupid to put herself in the middle? She'd tried today, without any luck at all.

She turned up her own walk, her feet dragging, wanting only to collapse on her own bed and turn up the stereo loud enough to blast away all the worries and doubts and suspicions. If there was any way she could believe that Jamey's bruises were the result of an accident . . . but she had seen the belt. The excuses were getting thinner, even to her own ears.

When she walked inside the foyer, she heard her mom call from beyond the kitchen. "Lauri, that you?"

"Yes," Lauri answered, walking through the kitchen and on into the laundry room.

Her mother stood over a pile of dirty laundry. "If you have anything else that needs washing, bring it here right now," her mom said. "Those jeans, for example. We're both running out of clothes, and I want to wash full loads and not waste water or energy. And hurry, so I can start dinner."

"Okay," Lauri agreed. She went back to her room and stripped, pulling on the long t-shirt she often slept in. She brought her jeans and shirt back to drop onto the pile, then returned to her room to study.

In a little while the aroma of cooking beef drifted into her room, and her empty stomach reminded her of how hungry she was. Lauri shut her book and wandered into the kitchen.

But her mother leaned against the counter, her expression twisted, holding a crumpled sheet of paper. There was the faint smell of beef in the air, and on the stove, Lauri saw half-cooked hamburger patties cooling in a pan.

"What's the matter?" Lauri asked. Then she recognized the sheet, and her breath caught in her throat. It was the list of family counsellors Mr. Dugan had given her. She'd forgotten to take it out of her jeans pocket.

Her mother looked up; the paper wavered in her hands.

"Lauri, is something wrong?" Her mother stared at her, then blinked hard. "I mean, you're not into drugs or drinking secretly—"

"Or course not," Lauri interrupted, not sure whether to laugh or cry. "I'm not that stupid."

"Are you unhappy?" Her mother turned to face her, her voice strained. "Is it me? I know I haven't been the best mother, and I—"

"Oh, no, Mom," Lauri blurted. "It's nothing like that. I just wanted to ask him about Jamey." Then she put one hand to her mouth. She hadn't meant to tell anyone, certainly not her mother, why she'd gone to the counsellor.

Her mother's face turned white, and she blinked in shock. "Lauri, you didn't tell anyone that you suspect your own uncle of child abuse? How could you?"

"No, Mom, I didn't. I just wanted to ask—I thought Mr. Dugan would know—but I never got the chance. I didn't say anything," Lauri said quickly, alarmed at her mother's expression.

"You know it's not true. . . ." her mother said, still gulping for air as if she'd been underwater too long, her arms now wrapped around her own body as if she needed the support.

"But I saw the bruises, the cuts. . . ." Lauri said, forcing the words out. "I found a belt in the bottom of Uncle Jack's closet—"

"Everybody wears belts, Lauri, for goodness sake. I refuse to believe that my own brother would—and what were you doing in his closet?"

Her mother wasn't going to listen, Lauri thought. It didn't matter what she said. She felt very tired.

"It's okay," she said now. "I didn't say anything,

really, to Mr. Dugan, and he never even spoke to Jamey.''

"You took Jamey with you?'' her mother's voice rose, and she was shouting suddenly. "Don't you know what you're doing—stirring up trouble just when I thought we might hang on to our home? When Jack finds out that you took Jamey in to see a shrink without asking—without anyone's permission—''

"He's not a shrink—a psychiatrist, I mean—he's a school counsellor, and he didn't talk to Jamey. And Jamey won't tell.''

"He's just a little boy, of course he will.'' Her mom pushed her auburn hair back and took another gasping breath. Just watching her made Lauri's chest ache.

"He didn't even know why we went to the high school,'' she said, her voice low. "And anyhow, I think Jamey's good at keeping secrets.''

"Stop it, stop it!'' Her mother took another wavering breath. She walked into the living room, sitting down suddenly onto the couch and pushing her hair back from her face. "Jack is crazy about Jamey, don't you see that? He talks about him all the time. And he's been so good to us, helping us with money when I really needed it. I couldn't make it without his help; we couldn't make it. We'll lose our house, Lauri.''

She was very pale, and a tear slipped down her cheek, while the dark mascara that rimmed her eyelids had smudged, leaving her brown eyes looking heavy and forlorn.

"I'm sorry, Mom,'' Lauri said, feeling her stomach clutch into knots of pain. "I didn't mean to cause trouble. I'm sorry. I don't think Uncle Jack will find out, honest.''

"Just don't say anything else about this, Lauri," her mother said. "Promise me."

She didn't understand, Lauri thought. Her mom hadn't seen the belt, hadn't felt Jamey hold her hand so tight when she was about to leave the apartment, as if he didn't want to let her go.

Her mom wiped her eyes, smearing the makeup even more. She wasn't going to listen, Lauri realized; her own fear was too great.

"I won't," Lauri said. "Don't worry, okay?"

She turned and ran to her room, pulling the door shut behind her. She'd made her mother cry, she hadn't helped Jamey at all, and it didn't look as if she would, or could. Even Karen thought Lauri was going to get in trouble if she kept on.

And Mac didn't even want to talk to her. She had no one to turn to, now.

CHAPTER FOURTEEN

Friday morning Lauri could hardly drag herself out of bed. A soon as she opened her eyes and remembered the disastrous events of the day before, a weight seemed to descend on her whole body. She felt weighed down, trapped in a gray cloud of despair. Nothing would help; she could do nothing without causing more harm.

She finally pulled on some jeans and a sweater, but she didn't have the energy to put on makeup or comb her hair. Her mom had already left for work. There were cinnamon buns on the kitchen counter, but Lauri's stomach still roiled, and the thought of food made her shudder. She trudged to the high school and discovered she was ten minutes late to her first class. When the next hour brought her geometry test, she stared blankly at the test sheet, trying to make the words and diagrams make sense. But her brain seemed somewhere else—she had the sense she was moving in slow motion—and it took great effort just to lift her pencil. When the period ended, she had made little progress, and she turned in the test with the page only half-filled.

As the bell rang, she gathered her things and put the incomplete test sheet on the teacher's desk, too depressed to care what she'd done to her math average. When she reached the hall, an even worse thought hit her. Psych class—no way could she face Mr. Dugan today! What if he asked her more about the "family problem" that she had muttered about yesterday? Just the thought of his gaze intent on her face made her fearful. She'd promised her mother she would say nothing more. If she got nervous and blurted out the wrong thing—no, no, not now, not so soon. She might have to face her teacher again, but not today, not this week. Thank heavens it was Friday.

She turned away from the psych classroom and headed for the library, instead. By rights, she needed a pass to spend the hour in the library, but she found a study cartel half-hidden among the rows of bookshelves, and no one asked to see her release from class. She stared blindly at a reference book until the hour was over, then she could go to lunch.

The smell of food—chicken tacos, greasy and strong—made her stomach lurch, and Lauri paused in the doorway to the cafeteria.

"Hey, out of the way," a boy behind her said.

Lauri moved aside.

"Lauri, where have you been? What's wrong? You look like my dad when he gets seasick," a familiar voice said. Karen took her arm and Lauri leaned against her. "What's up? And why didn't you come to psych class?"

"I don't—I don't feel well," Lauri said. "Did Mr. Dugan say anything?"

"He asked me if you were at school, and I said I

hadn't seen you this morning, which was true,'' Karen said. ''Come on, sit down, and I'll get you something to eat.''

''I don't think I can,'' Lauri told her, but a wave of light-headedness made her afraid to let go of Karen's arm. ''The smells are too strong—I think I'm going to throw up or pass out, I don't know which.''

Her friend steered her to a table, and Lauri sat down abruptly in the closest chair.

''You're as white as my mom's best towels. When was the last time you ate?'' Karen demanded.

''I—I don't know,'' Lauri said slowly, suddenly remembering that after the awful blowup with her mother, she'd never gone back to eat dinner. No wonder her knees were weak and the lunchroom seemed to sway and dip around her. She put one hand to her head and tried to keep the room from spinning.

''I'll be right back,'' Karen said, dropping her backpack on the chair next to Lauri. ''You stay here; don't try to walk by yourself.''

Lauri felt as if her legs wouldn't hold her up, so the warning was unnecessary. She shut her eyes and breathed through her mouth, trying not to smell the spicy tacos, which only made her feel nauseous. ''No tacos,'' she muttered, but Karen was already on her way toward the food lines.

Her friend returned in a few minutes, and she held out a tray with a bowl of soup and a pile of crackers.

''Try this,'' Karen said. ''The vegetable soup is usually pretty good, and I got you some cola, too, which might help your stomach.''

Lauri looked at the food. ''I don't know if I can,'' she said, swallowing again.

"You need to," Karen said, her expression concerned. "Take small bites and eat slowly. Just try, okay? If you can't eat, I'm going to take you to the school nurse."

Lauri shook her head at the threat, which only made her head spin again—as if she were strong enough to resist anything at the moment, she thought wryly—but she picked up the spoon and dipped it into the red broth. She took a tiny bite, then another. The salty, tomato broth of the soup tasted good, and the diced vegetables were tender. As she ate slowly, her stomach began to calm.

She was able to eat most of the soup and crackers, and when she pushed the tray back, she looked across to her friend. Karen was eating salad and a baked potato—no tacos, though they were one of her favorite lunches.

True friendship, Lauri thought ruefully, remembering how she had lashed out at Karen not so long ago.

"Thanks," she said. "For everything."

Karen shrugged. "No problem. You want to tell me what this is all about?"

Lauri sighed. "I tried to take Jamey to see Mr. Dugan yesterday."

"You didn't?" Karen's eyes widened. "What happened?"

"Nothing," Lauri told her. "He said he couldn't talk to him without the permission of his parents."

"What did your uncle say?"

Lauri shuddered despite herself. "He doesn't know, and I hope he doesn't find out! It was bad enough my mom does know, and she had a fit—she said I was going to make us lose the house. . . ." Lauri's voice faltered and she looked away from her friend's sympathetic gaze. "I—I just made a mess of everything, that's all."

"You were trying to help," Karen said. "Once your mother calms down, maybe—"

Lauri shook her head. "She won't listen—can't, maybe. She freaks out when she thinks we'll lose the house. It's like her security blanket, I think. And I don't like the thought, either. It's my home, too, you know."

Karen nodded.

"And now I have to go on like nothing's happened, and every time I see my uncle, I get nervous . . . and I don't know how to help Jamey. And then"— Lauri plunged on, toying with a piece of cracker—"there's Mac."

"What about him—did you guys talk?" Karen asked, her tone hopeful.

Lauri shook her head. "No, I saw him in the hall with another girl—really cute, too. Long, blonde hair and big blue eyes—the Barbie type, you know."

"Oh, not good," Karen agreed. "Boys eat that up. When I was dating Carlos last year . . ."

As her friend talked about boys, Lauri looked down and found that her grip had tightened until the cracker crumbled in her fingers. She wiped her hands and tried to keep her expression even. In a way, it was easier to talk about her failed love life. As much as it hurt to have Mac out of reach, she knew deep down that Jamey's situation was much more perilous.

At least after eating, she felt stronger physically, and when the lunch period ended, she could walk to her next class and was able to survive the rest of the school day. When she had to walk the few blocks to the elementary school, she almost dreaded seeing Jamey, afraid something else would have occurred to jog her guilty conscience. But he was waiting at the classroom door, wearing his T-ball shirt, his jacket unzipped and his small backpack hung over one arm.

"Let's go," he said at once. "I can't be late to the game!"

Lauri nodded, and today they walked straight to the park. His teammates were already gathered on the ball field. Jamey dropped his pack and jacket at her feet and ran eagerly on to join his friends.

The nearest benches were full, so Lauri sat down on the grass a little way from the field, behind a trio of mothers who had also come to watch the game.

She knew she was hiding from Mac, but didn't regret her cowardly impulse. Today was not the best day for more confrontations; she didn't have the energy.

When Mac was turned toward the players, she could look his way safely without fear that he would glance up and catch her gaze. She watched as Mac helped Jamey don the protective headgear and step up to the T-ball frame.

Jamey swung hard at the ball, whacking it with a satisfying thunk that sent it flying across the ball field. He dropped the bat and ran doggedly down the baseline. The first baseman, a petite redhead, reached for the ball and missed, and Jamey trotted on to second base, then third.

Lauri jumped to her feet, excited despite herself. "Run Jamey, run!" she called.

One of the boys from the other team had finally stopped the rolling ball; in his excitement, he dropped it twice, then threw it toward home. But the ball sailed too high, over the pint-sized catcher's head and into the waiting players, who milled around in confusion as everyone tried to grab the ball.

Jamey sailed across home plate, his smile wide.

Lauri clapped hard and yelled, "Way to go, Jamey! Home run!" Laughing out loud, she watched half of his own team run off the field to clap him on the back, while some of the opposing team forgot their allegiance and joined in the impromptu celebration.

Jamey turned to beam at her, and she held up her hand to give him the victory sign. Then she looked past the little boy and saw Mac grinning at her.

For an instant, she smiled back, then—confused—she looked down at the grass and sat back down, trying to lose herself behind the other spectators. By the time she looked up again, Mac was busy with his players.

The game continued. The next time he came up to bat, Jamey got another base hit, and then later was tagged out twice, but his enjoyment of the game seemed unabated. When his team won safely by three runs, all the players cheered and jumped up and down, and they lined up to shake hands good-naturedly with the losing team.

Then they clustered around Mac, still chattering with excitement. Lauri waited, not wanting to approach the circle of players. Would Jamey ever emerge from the knot of sweaty, red-faced, grinning little kids? Eventually, she picked up his pack and his jacket and wandered just a little closer.

Jamey saw her and ran to tug on her arm. "Tim and Juan and Hak Lin are going to get a pizza with their moms. Can we go, too?"

Lauri glanced at her watch. "I'm sorry, Jamey. We'd

better not. I didn't tell your dad we'd be late, and he won't know where we are.''

Jamey's grin faded, and he looked down, scuffing the dirt with his sneakers. ''Oh,'' he said.

She hated to see his happiness fade so quickly. ''But you played a wonderful game, Jamey. I was so proud of you.''

''Honest?'' He looked back at her and his lips curved upward again. ''Nobody else made a home run, huh?''

''No, indeed,'' Lauri told him.

Then a shadow touched Jamey's small frame, and Lauri looked up to see Mac standing beside him.

''Good game, Jamey,'' Mac told the little boy. ''We've beaten all the local park teams, so don't forget the extra game on Monday; we get to play the crosstown park champions now.''

''Oh, boy,'' Jamey said. ''I won't be late. We won't be late Monday, right, Lauri?''

''Right,'' Lauri said, blushing a little. She couldn't seem to meet Mac's gaze, it was so level, his brown eyes so clear.

''Jamey, why don't you go tell the others not to be late on Monday, okay?'' Mac asked.

''But you already told them,'' Jamey pointed out.

Lauri tried not to giggle. This time, Mac turned slightly red.

''I know, but just remind them one more time,'' he told the little boy.

Jamey nodded and walked back across to the shrinking knot of players.

''Kids,'' Mac said, watching him. ''They don't take a hint very well.''

''No,'' Lauri agreed. She kept her expression bland

with great effort, but inside, she felt her pulse jump. Why would Mac want to speak to her alone, if it wasn't about the two of them—if he didn't still care, a little?

She found that he was looking at her seriously; he still stood very close, and she took a deep breath.

"Are you—are you seeing that other girl?" she blurted, then felt her cheeks burn. That wasn't at all what she'd meant to say.

"What girl?" Mac blinked in surprise.

"I saw you in the hall, talking to a—a pretty blonde," Lauri dropped her gaze to stare at Mac's tightly-laced athletic shoes. "I thought, maybe—"

"Oh, you mean Roberta," Mac said. "We're doing a chem project together, that's all."

"Oh," Lauri said, still not sure she wanted to look him in the face. Maybe he would see too much in her eyes. Maybe he would think she wanted him back. Maybe he would be right.

"Lauri, I just wondered—if you still—if you'd thought about—" Mac was stammering. "A-about us. If you wanted to try again?"

Maybe she wasn't the only one whose stomach went into knots and whose tongue refused to work. Maybe Mac did care.

For a moment hope soared inside her, then all the weight of her dark secret rushed back. There was too much they couldn't discuss, too many suspicions that had to remain in the shadows. She'd promised her mom not to talk about Jamey anymore, and Mac would be the first person to see that she was worried, to notice if Jamey showed up with more bruises. It was too much to risk.

"I—I can't," she said, looking away.

There was silence for a moment, and then Mac spoke very quietly.

"Right. So, sorry I asked. I just thought—I liked you the first time I saw you. I guess I thought—in time—we might have had something special."

He turned quickly and moved back to say good-bye to the last of the T-ball players, then bent to collect the equipment into the dusty canvas bag. So he couldn't have seen Lauri blink hard against the tears that flooded her eyes and blurred her view of him.

"We would have," she whispered. "I just know it." Then she coughed to clear the lump in her throat and waved to her cousin.

"Jamey, come on," she called.

The little boy ran to her side, and they walked slowly, silently, out of the park.

CHAPTER FIFTEEN

When they reached Jamey's apartment, Lauri unlocked the door and led the way inside.

"I'm thirsty," Jamey told her.

"Would you like some juice?" she asked.

When he nodded, she poured him a glass. He sat down at the table and drank his juice very carefully. The excitement of the game seemed to have faded; he acted subdued and turned down her offer of a board game, flipping on the television instead.

It wasn't long until Uncle Jack came in. He looked tired, his tie was already loosened and his eyes bloodshot, and he seemed impatient for Lauri to leave. He had her check already made out, and when she murmured a thank-you, he hardly seemed to notice.

"Want to order a pizza, Sport?" he asked his son.

"Sure," Jamey agreed and ran across to hug Lauri good-bye. He threw his arms around her neck and held her even tighter than usual.

"You'll come back tomorrow?" he whispered.

"Tomorrow is Saturday, Jamey," she reminded him, keeping her voice low. "I'll see you on Monday, don't worry."

She thought for a moment he wasn't going to let go, his grip was almost a stranglehold. "It's a long time till Monday," he whispered again.

Lauri hugged him one more time, then gently put him aside so she could straighten her aching back. "Have fun this weekend," she told him.

Throwing her backpack over one arm, Lauri said good-bye and walked slowly home. She couldn't seem to forget her last glimpse of Jamey, peering at her through the half-open door, his expression still troubled.

A dark thought blossomed in the back of her mind, like a cloud of noxious smoke, and wouldn't go away.

What happened on the weekends?

Nothing, nothing, nothing, she told herself furiously. So, Jamey missed her. They got along pretty well, didn't they? She played games with him and took him to the park; his father maybe didn't have the patience to play with his son. It didn't mean Jamey was mistreated. She had to forget what she'd thought about before—she might be wrong. Most of all, she'd promised her mother—and Jamey was okay, Jamey would be okay. She'd see him Monday after school, and they'd go to the park and play all his favorite games.

There was nothing else she could do, nothing at all.

When she got home, she found her mother in the kitchen, and good smells of food in the air. Lauri tossed her jacket into the hall closet and dropped her backpack. She walked on into the kitchen. On the stove, chicken sizzled in a pan of hot fat, and potatoes bubbled in another saucepan. The aroma made Lauri's mouth water. She looked at her mother in surprise.

"You didn't go out with Jean?" she said. On Friday evenings, her mother and one or more friends often stopped for a drink at a cocktail lounge after work.

Her mother shook her head. "I wanted to cook you something decent, for a change. And anyhow, I've decided not to throw away the money. After all, you're giving me all your wages for baby-sitting Jamey. . . ."

Lauri felt embarrassed. "I don't mind," she said, and it was mostly true. "You needed it for the house payments." She took out the latest check and put it on the counter. "Here's the one Uncle Jack gave me today."

Her mother nodded. "Yes, we do need it, I'm sorry to say. But I have an extra day to work this week. I'm working tomorrow until two o'clock; we're giving flu shots at the clinic. I'll get time and a half, and it will make a nice extra bonus in my paycheck. And as soon as I get home, we're going straight to the mall and buy you a new outfit."

"Really?" Lauri couldn't help feeling pleased, but then she hesitated. "If you have extra money this week, shouldn't we save it?"

"Probably," her mother agreed, smiling a bit ruefully as she picked up a spatula and carefully turned the chicken. "But I can't have my daughter going naked, either. You have to have new clothes once in a while."

Lauri laughed, glancing down at her much worn jeans and tee shirt. "I guess."

"Wash up," her mother told her. "I'll mash the potatoes and make gravy, and we'll be ready to eat soon."

Dinner was relaxed, and they chatted about inconsequential topics. No one mentioned Jamey's name, and when her mother asked about her day at school, Lauri said, "It was okay," and pushed aside the thought of the geometry test. If she admitted how poorly she thought she'd done on the exam, she'd have to explain why she'd been upset and unable to concentrate, and that would take them right back to Jamey and Uncle Jack. It was like forbidden ground, and even thinking about her little cousin made her mouthful of potatoes harder to swallow.

Not now, not now, she told herself fiercely. She loved her mom's mashed potatoes, they were her very favorite. *Just eat, don't think, don't worry. . . .*

After dinner, she helped her mom clean up the kitchen, scrubbing off the splatters of grease that dotted the stove, and then went back to her room for a while to try to study that dratted math. She had to make up for the disastrous test score, somehow. Like Mac, she too might try for a scholarship some day. But thinking of Mac hurt, too.

Lauri tossed her textbook across the bed in a sudden fit of temper. It hit the wall with a resounding thwack, then fell to the carpet. Lauri sighed and went around the bed to pick it up again. Getting angry didn't help.

She lay back against her pillows, glancing up now and then at the familiar white curtains and the prints on the wall, her mother's face in the photo by the bed. Her room, her house. She had to stand by her mother; who did they have but each other? When the men in your family always left—

Unwillingly, Lauri remembered what Karen had said. Was that the reason—or one of the reasons—she had broken up with Mac so soon? Was it easier to leave before you really cared about someone, before he had the chance to leave you?

Lauri bit her lip, feeling a quick wave of emotion that took her by surprise. When her father had left—remembering that time was like being submerged in a current of darkness, of emptiness and pain. She rolled over and pushed her hands to her face, trying to stop the memories. Drat Karen, anyhow, and drat Mr. Dugan. She wished she hadn't even started this whole psych class business. She would have been happier if she didn't know—

No, what did Mr. Dugan say? Understanding the problem was the first step, then you could do something about it.

Which led her thoughts right back to Jamey, whose problem—no, darn it, she couldn't think about Jamey, either.

She pushed herself up on her elbows and reached across to flip the switch on her clock radio. She turned to her favorite rock station and turned the volume up high.

The music washed over her, and she lay back against her pillow, trying to lose herself in the words, the rhythm, letting it drown out any conscious thought at all. She lay there holding her extra pillow tightly over her face, hiding behind it as if it were a stuffed animal, like the large shaggy teddy bear she'd owned when she was small. In a few minutes, her mother pounded on her bedroom door.

"Turn it down, Lauri!"

Lauri reached across and lowered the volume, but she listened to the music till at last, after a small eternity, she fell into a troubled sleep.

• • •

Saturday morning Lauri slept late, and woke feeling sluggish and still tired. Her mom had already left for the clinic, and Lauri ate a piece of toast and an orange, then cleaned house. By the time her mom came home from work, she'd showered and changed into clean clothes, excited about the shopping trip despite her many worries. It had been a long time since she'd had new clothes, new anything. Her mom came in the door smiling.

"How'd all the flu shots go?" Lauri asked, watching her mom take a laundry bag full of the white lab coats she wore at work and drop them onto the washing machine.

"Hectic, but I'm free now," her mother said merrily. "Let me wash my face and hands and we're off."

They drove to the mall and spent several hours cruising Lauri's favorite shops. She tried on numerous pieces, unable to keep from almost obsessively checking the price tags, which she never even used to notice. After long searching, she finally found a blouse and skirt that she really liked, and which had been marked down, which made her feel less guilty about the purchase.

"Don't you like them?" she asked her mom, who looked her up and down as Lauri modeled the outfit in front of the three-way mirror.

"The color's good on you," her mother agreed. "Are you sure they wear skirts that short at the high school?"

"Oh, Mom, it's the style," Lauri protested.

Her mother smiled. "I suppose. Okay, you look terrific."

They stood in line at the cash register, and then Lauri walked out with a shopping bag on one arm.

Her mom glanced across at an ice cream shop. "Don't those sundaes look good."

"Let's get one," Lauri suggested, aware of how hungry she was.

Her mother glanced at her watch. "I don't know; it's almost time for dinner."

"So, let's spoil our appetites," Lauri coaxed. "It's Saturday!"

Her mother laughed. "Oh, why not?"

She went up to get their order while Lauri sat down at one of the small, white tables. It was great to see her mother relaxed for once, Lauri thought. She looked across at the other customers and saw a small boy licking his spoon, his face smeared with chocolate syrup, and she thought about Jamey. What was he doing this Saturday afternoon? Was he laughing, too, or—

No, Jamey was okay, she told herself, as if repeating the refrain often enough to herself would make it come true. He was okay; he had to be okay.

Her mother came back with two sundaes and gave Lauri her favorite, chocolate caramel. But she ate it slowly, some of her enjoyment gone.

At least the ice cream gave her an excuse not to talk, to nod and smile as her mother talked to her about work, about a class at the business school she was thinking of taking.

"If I had more training, I might make a better salary," her mother explained. "After all, we have college coming up for you before too long."

Lauri was surprised enough to put down her spoon. "You think we can afford it?"

"We have to," her mother told her, her tone suddenly determined. "You have to have a better life than I have,

Sweetie. I want you to get a good job, and not to have to worry about bills getting paid, or losing your own home. And that means an education.''

"But . . .'' Lauri stared at her mother. Maybe the last few months had made more impact on her mother than she'd realized. Her mom was sounding, at times, more— more like a real parent. Then Lauri looked down at her sundae and smiled. Okay, so having ice cream for dinner was not totally responsible, but still . . .

"What's so funny?'' her mother demanded.

"You have caramel sauce on your nose,'' Lauri told her, watching her mother grab a napkin hastily. Some things didn't change.

After a leisurely Sunday brunch of pancakes and sausage the next morning, one of her mother's friends called to say she had an extra ticket for a Home Show, and wanted to know if her mom wanted to come.

"Sounds like fun,'' her mother agreed. "I'll be ready when you come by.'' She hung up the phone and looked across at Lauri. "You don't mind?''

"Of course not,'' Lauri told her. "I might go over to Karen's.''

She found a sweater to pull over her tee shirt—the day was balmy—and walked over to her friend's house. But she found Karen also getting ready to go out.

"We're having dinner at my uncle and aunt's in Encino. Want to come? I can ask my mom,'' Karen told her as she helped her sister button her sweater.

"No, that's okay, just thought you might want to hang out,'' Lauri said. "Have fun.''

"Ha, great fun, listening to Martin count license

plates and hoping Angie doesn't get carsick on the way and throw up on me again.'' Karen made a face.

Lauri walked outside with her friend and watched as Karen and her parents loaded the younger kids into the family van.

"You know you have to wear your seat belt, Martin," Karen told her brother. "Now don't give me any lip!"

Grinning, Lauri waved good-bye when the van pulled out of the driveway.

Now what? She walked slowly toward home. Seeing Karen's siblings reminded her once more of Jamey. He'd complained about how long the weekend was, poor kid. What was he doing now?

She paused at the corner of the next street and suddenly changed directions. Surely she could drop in at Jamey's apartment just for a minute. She could offer to take her cousin to the park for a while; Uncle Jack would appreciate the gesture. And she didn't have anything better to do this afternoon, that was for sure.

She walked more quickly now and knew suddenly that she'd been wanting to do this all weekend. Even yesterday, she really wouldn't have minded having Jamey along on their shopping trip to the mall. He'd probably have complained about all the women's clothing shops, most little kids would, but he was such a good kid, really. How could anyone get so angry at Jamey that—that—

She was back in the forbidden zone again, those thoughts she had promised herself to put out of her head. She took long, quick strides, almost running, and soon saw Jamey's apartment complex ahead of her.

She didn't have Jamey's key today and could hardly have walked into the apartment uninvited, anyhow. She rang the bell instead and waited impatiently for some noise, some sign that someone was coming to answer.

Had Uncle Jack and Jamey gone out? Maybe they were at the park, and the little boy was playing happily. All her worry had probably been for nothing.

Then she heard a noise behind the closed door, and the door swung open a few inches. She saw her uncle peering at her.

"Lauri? What's up?"

"Can I come in?" she said, wondering if he would open the door further.

Slowly, her uncle swung the door back and Lauri walked into the apartment.

Her uncle looked different on a weekend. He had on jeans and a knit shirt, instead of the usual business suit and tie, and he hadn't shaved. A half-filled bottle of whiskey sat on the coffee table, along with an almost empty glass. The air in the apartment smelled stale, and a ball game blared from the television screen. She saw no sign of Jamey.

"So?" her uncle repeated. Was he slurring his words just slightly? "Something wrong at home?"

"No, no, I just th—thought—" Lauri felt self-conscious suddenly and found herself stammering. "I—I just wondered, maybe you'd like me to take Jamey to the park for a while?"

"Jamey's grounded. He didn't pick up his toys," her uncle said.

Lauri glanced around; she saw one small toy car and two coloring books on the floor, then she looked down the hallway; Jamey's bedroom door was firmly shut. "But it would be good for him to—"

Her uncle shook his head.

Lauri felt panicky suddenly. Jamey was so close, and she couldn't see him, couldn't be sure that he was okay. "Could I just say hello?" she insisted. She took a deep breath, trying to stay calm.

Again, her uncle shook his head, and now he frowned. "I told you, he's being punished. Don't interfere, hear me?"

"I just—"

"What, does Marietta need more money already?" Her uncle made a motion as if to reach for his wallet, and Lauri flushed.

"No, no, nothing like that. I just wanted to see Jamey, to make sure—to make sure he was okay."

Her uncle paused, and the silence was suddenly tense. "Why wouldn't he be?" he demanded, his voice a little too loud.

This time, Lauri met his gaze. Her stomach felt hollow, and her knees had gone weak, but she didn't look away. "I saw his back," she said clearly.

Silence again, and she thought her uncle's lips tightened. Then he thrust out one hand and grabbed her shoulder before she could back away. He pulled her a step closer, and he was too strong to resist.

His grip was very powerful; her shoulder hurt from the pressure of his hand. She felt small, all at once, and powerless, and her mouth went dry. He wouldn't hit her, he couldn't—could he?

"Don't push your nose in where it doesn't belong," her uncle said, his voice thick with anger. They stood so close now that she could smell the whiskey heavy on his breath, and see the red veins that streaked the white of his eyes. "Just 'cause you're baby-sitting Jamey, that don't make you his mother. So butt out, you hear me?"

Had Jamey's mother complained about the way Jack had treated their son?

Lauri took a deep breath, almost choking on the smell of liquor, but she was too frightened to answer, to say any of the thoughts that rushed through her head.

What had he done to Jamey, this time? Oh, Jamey.

Her uncle released her as suddenly as he'd grabbed her and pulled open the door. "I'll see you Monday," he told her. "And Lauri—"

She looked at him numbly, still unable to trust her voice. She didn't want it to quaver with fear, didn't want to give him that satisfaction.

"You keep your mouth shut. You don't want to cause your own family trouble, right? And you sure don't want to lose your house. Remember that."

She was outside, though she couldn't remember how she'd gotten there, staring at the closed door. She stood there for a long time, just looking at the apartment entrance. Where was Jamey? Was he crying in his bedroom? Had he been *punished* again?

Ohgodohgodohgod, what could she do?

At last she turned toward home, walking the long blocks without seeing any of the buildings around her, vaguely surprised when she reached her own house. She looked at the familiar stucco structure as if she'd never noticed it before. She let herself in—her mom wasn't home yet, thank goodness—and went to her bedroom, shutting the door and looking around her.

She still felt dazed. She looked around her bedroom, then sank to the floor next to her bed as her knees seemed to give way of their own accord. She sat on the soft, plush carpet and hugged her knees. All this they would lose, if she told anyone what she suspected—no, what she knew. Would her mom ever forgive her? How could she double-cross her own mother. . . .

Later, she slipped off her sweater and looked in the mirror; her uncle's grip had left finger-sized red marks on her skin. The area was still sore, but the marks were fading fast. Lauri thought about showing her mom—if she could only understand—but then she shivered, thinking about what her uncle would say.

And yet, and yet, she remembered the fear that had washed over her when Uncle Jack had held her, and how powerless she had felt—like a puppet, helpless, at his mercy. If she felt like that, how must Jamey feel when his father turned against him?

When her mother got home, Lauri said little to her. She stayed in her room all evening, pretending to study. She was relieved when her mother went to bed early and turned out the light.

Lauri lay on her bed in the darkness, staring at the dark silhouettes of furniture against the paler wall, while dim light from the streetlight edged past her curtains. She knew this room even in the dark, and she felt a deep sadness at the thought of giving it up.

But Jamey was out there, alone, and he was hurting. She knew it; she was sure of it, deep inside her. No matter what happened to Lauri, to her mom, someone had to think about Jamey first. Who cared about Jamey's pain? If he wept, silent and alone, who would cry for him?

And at some point in the night, she knew what she had to do.

CHAPTER SIXTEEN

The next morning Lauri took her time getting ready, staying in her bathroom till her mom had left for work, after calling a cheerful good-bye to her daughter through the door.

Her mother sounded so at ease, so normal. What would she say to Lauri the next time she saw her? Would she ever forgive her? Lauri didn't want to face her mother this morning; she felt like a traitor, and she was afraid it would show in her face.

Later, she walked quickly to school, but she moved through her classes like a robot, hardly aware of what was going on around her.

Even in psych class, she only glanced at Mr. Dugan. Next to her other worries, her fear of what he might think or say seemed a small thing.

In fact, he called her name as she was about to leave the classroom. ''Ms. Whitley, could you wait just a moment?''

She walked up to his desk, too numb to be afraid any longer.

Mr. Dugan gave her a thoughtful look. "If you need to talk, Ms. Whitley, I'm here any time," he told her, his hazel eyes friendly but intent. "You left the office in such a hurry the other day, I was concerned."

"Yes, thanks," she muttered. "I'll remember." Hitching her backpack more firmly over one arm, she headed for the hallway. Why had she been so afraid of her teacher? He couldn't read her mind, after all. And he couldn't do what she had to do, because she was the one who knew about Jamey's secret pain.

Karen caught up with her in the hallway. "What's wrong with you?" she asked. "You haven't heard a word I've said to you today."

"Nothing," Lauri said.

But after they'd gone through the food line and sat down at one of the tables, Karen persisted. "I mean it, Lauri, what's wrong?"

"What makes you think something's wrong?" Lauri dipped a spoon into the soup and sipped cautiously. She didn't need to be weak from hunger today; she would need all her strength, physical and mental.

"Oh, come off it," Karen snapped. "You can talk to me, you know."

But she didn't know. Lauri swallowed the soup and wouldn't meet her best friend's eyes.

"What are you thinking about? At least give me a clue," Karen begged.

This time Lauri laughed a little wildly. "Patrick Henry, Martin Luther King Jr., Joan of Arc."

"What?" Karen looked even more bewildered. "Do you have a new history project? Is that all?"

Lauri shrugged. "Not exactly. It's about—about

having the courage of your convictions, and then—then taking the consequences. . . ."

"But . . ." Karen blinked in confusion, and Lauri shook her head.

"I'll tell you later, I promise. I'm just not ready to talk about it right now, okay?"

"I guess," Karen grumbled. But she picked up her sandwich and took a bite. "I think I may have to visit you in the loony bin, the way you're acting this week."

"Maybe," Lauri agreed. Or maybe in jail, she thought grimly.

The afternoon stretched on for years, but at last the final bell sounded. Lauri left her books in her locker and hurried for the outside door. She was one of the first students to sprint down the front steps, and she almost ran for the elementary school.

At last, at last she could see Jamey, see his face light up when he saw her coming, hug him gently and check for more bruises. And then—she'd made up her mind during the night—then they were going to find a police station. She had looked up the address of the closest station in the phone book before leaving home, and she would tell the police that she thought Jamey was being abused by his father.

And then, surely, surely, someone would have to check, to investigate, to look at Jamey's body for old bruises or new ones, to do some intense scrutiny of Uncle Jack. Someone with authority, with power, whom Jack couldn't overawe or physically threaten.

And if her uncle blamed it all on Lauri—she'd have to take that chance. If her mother was angry—Lauri swallowed hard at the thought. That was even worse than thinking of the possibility of jail for herself. Worse than losing their house.

It had always been just her mom, just the two of them, really, despite the men in her mom's life who had come and gone. If her mother hated her—

She had to do it, for Jamey's sake.

The walk to the elementary school had never seemed so long, even though she loped down the sidewalk and waited impatiently, shifting from one foot to the other, at every light. When she saw the school, she hurried down the open-air walkway to find Jamey's classroom.

Most of the children were still pushing books into their desks or claiming jackets and sweaters from the hooks on the far wall. But where was Jamey?

Lauri felt the tension rise inside her when she looked at his desk. It was neat and clean and bare.

Where was Jamey?

She looked around the room, trying not to panic. Surely her uncle hadn't kept him at home today? Uncle Jack must have gone to work. She should have skipped school entirely and come to the elementary school first thing this morning. But she'd been afraid the teacher wouldn't let her take him away. She should have . . . oh, she should have done so much differently.

Lauri looked around again, hoping against hope that Jamey would suddenly appear, that he had been to the bathroom, on an errand for the teacher, anything.

The teacher—Lauri turned to the front of the class and stared at the woman sitting behind the desk. Surely that wasn't Jamey's teacher? What was her name? Lauri hurried up to the desk.

A small name plaque on the top of the desk jogged Lauri's memory. "Mrs. Vaughn?" she asked.

The young woman finished tying a little girl's bow and turned to Lauri. "No, I'm Ms. Elliot. Mrs. Vaughn had to leave suddenly today; I'm a substitute who was called in to take her place. Can I help you?"

"Oh," Lauri said. "Do you—do you know if Jamey Barron was in school today? I'm his cousin; I always pick him up after school."

"Oh," the teacher said. "I'm afraid the attendance list has already gone back to the central office, but I don't recall his name being on the absentee list. Of course, I don't know the children by sight, you know. Sorry."

"Thanks," Lauri said. She walked back outside and looked around again, still hoping that Jamey would appear magically out of the crowd of children who flowed along the walkway, heading home.

He always waited for her in the classroom. If he had been at school, why would he be anywhere else?

She headed for the central wing of the school, but when she glanced into the front office, a crowd of children and parents all seemed to be waiting to be helped.

Lauri swallowed, impatience jostling the anxiety inside her. Where was Jamey?

Then suddenly she remembered the extra T-ball game that was scheduled for today. Was it possible that Jamey was so excited about the game—so anxious not to be late—that he had started for the park on his own?

It seemed the likeliest explanation. Without wasting any more time at the school, she headed for the park, constantly scanning the sidewalks for Jamey's familiar figure. She was going to give him a scolding when she saw him, that was for sure. And how would she ever convince him to leave the game and go to the police station with her?

One thing at a time; first, she had to find him. Lauri hurried along the usual route, her heart jumping every time she saw a small figure with sandy hair. But every time she rushed up to call his name, another small face looked at her with expression of bewilderment or alarm, and she saw it was a different child.

"Sorry," Lauri murmured. Oh, where was Jamey?

When she reached the park entrance, Lauri sprinted on till she came to the ball field. Sure enough, the field was crowded with small ball players in colorful shirts, weaving amid the parents who adjusted gloves and tightened sneakers and gave last-minute advice.

Lauri looked from child to child, but she still couldn't make out Jamey. Where could he be?

She didn't want to speak to Mac, but this time, she would have to swallow her pride and ask for his help. Jamey always followed Mac around like a puppy.

However, she couldn't locate Mac, either, and he was always on the field early. Maybe he'd gone back inside the park gym building to fetch equipment and Jamey had tagged along. That made sense.

Lauri walked quickly across to the gym and looked inside the outer doors. A few children sat on the benches, but otherwise, it was deserted. She walked along the hardwood floor, her sneakers thudding softly on the hard surface, and found the office, but the door was locked.

Darn it, not today, she didn't need this today, just when she'd gotten her courage up to do what had to be done.

Lauri took a deep breath and turned toward the outside doors. Back on the field, she walked through the crowd of kids and parents, and this time, a scrap of conversation cut through her mental fog.

"A policeman came in a black-and-white patrol car and took him away—"

"And he seemed like such a nice boy," another mother said. "He was so good with the children. I was so astonished—"

Police? Lauri stopped in mid-stride, and her heart seemed to jump to her throat. She had to swallow hard before she could interrupt the two women.

"Who?" she demanded, her voice sounding raspy. "Who did the police take away?"

"Why, our T-ball coach, Mac—I forget his last name—" the woman told her, frowning. "Now they're saying he abused one of the children. I was aghast. You'd think the park authority would be more careful with the kids they hire—"

Not only Jamey was suffering now. Mac was being hurt, too.

"It—it's not true," Lauri stuttered, sick with shock. "It's not true!"

It had to be about Jamey. Had someone else reported the abuse? Had Uncle Jack decided to accuse someone else before Lauri could tell the police about him?

Otherwise, why had the police blamed Mac, of all people? She had to tell them—she had to explain—already, the team parents were believing the awful story. How could Mac ever live it down? And the thought of Mac in jail—for something he didn't do—there were tears on her cheeks, but she hardly noticed.

She ran for the street, pulling out the address of the police station from her jeans pocket and glancing at the street number. Oh, if only they would believe her!

When she found the right address, the police station was a neat brick building. Black-and-white police cars were parked along the side, and a man in a business suit came down the steps as she watched. She paused only a moment in front of the station, her stomach knotting in fear. It looked so official, so intimidating.

Then she took a deep breath and walked up the steps, pulling open the front door. A man in a blue uniform sat behind the front desk, his eyes on a stack of papers in front of him.

"Can I help you?" he asked, glancing at Lauri.

"They said at the park, you brought in Mac Emerson—he didn't do it!" she blurted.

"Can you start from the beginning, miss?" the officer asked mildly. "This is about—"

"It's about—it's about my cousin, really, Jamey Barron," Lauri said. "He's—I think he's being abused by his father. I was going to bring him to the police today, myself. And maybe he—my uncle—blamed it on Mac, I don't know, but you have to believe me, it wasn't Mac—"

She was crying for real, now, the tears running down her cheeks and stopping up her nose and making her voice squeak. Lauri rubbed at her face, hoping the man who watched her with such a noncommittal expression would listen, would believe her, wouldn't write her off as a hysterical teenager.

"Then we'd better find you the right person to talk to," the officer said calmly. He picked up a phone and spoke into it, then in a moment, said, "Second door on your right, please."

Lauri walked down the hall, ignoring several people in the hall who glanced curiously at her.

When she found the right door, she knocked timidly, not sure if she should open it.

"Come in," someone said.

Inside, a middle-aged black man with grizzled hair and a slight paunch sat behind the desk. "I understand you have information about the case of Jamey Barron?" he said.

"Yes, is he—is Jamey all right?" she said in a rush.

The policeman nodded. "He was taken to the hospital this morning," he told her.

"The hospital?" Lauri almost fell into the chair in front of the desk. "Is he okay?"

For a moment, the room seemed to darken and whirl around her, and she saw glints of light at the edges of her vision. She could barely make out the policeman as he stood up quickly and came around his desk.

"Put your head between your knees," he told her, his tone curt.

It seemed a strange thing to say, but she bent forward, her face down, and in a moment, the room steadied. When she could breathe again without feeling the tightness in her chest, she raised her head slowly.

The policeman shook his head. "I'm going to get you a soda," he said. "Just sit right there and don't try to stand up. I don't want you passing out on me."

"But—but Jamey, is he all right?" If her cousin had died, been seriously injured—how would she ever forgive herself for not acting more quickly?

The officer shook his head. "The little boy has a broken arm. His teacher discovered it this morning and took him straight to the hospital, where the doctor called in the police. When there's any question of possible child abuse, the hospitals have to notify the proper authorities. He's been put into the custody of Children's Services for the time being, until the case can be investigated."

Jamey with a broken bone, Jamey in the care of strangers. Yet hadn't his own family let him down? Lauri felt a wave of shame.

"He must be scared," she said, very low. "He's only six, you know. Can I see him, please, just talk to him?"

"We'll see," the officer told her. "Now, you sit still; I'll be right back."

She was too weak to move, even to protest. The policeman went out into the hall, leaving the door open. Lauri watched the hall for his return, but it was another familiar form that brought her to her feet.

"Mac!"

He stopped in surprise and she rushed to the door, still dizzy but so happy to see him, even with a policeman just behind him, that she threw her arms around him. He didn't push her away, but his body felt stiff as she clutched him.

"I came to tell them it wasn't you! It couldn't be you. Oh, Mac, I'm so sorry. I should have said something days ago, when I first suspected."

Mac looked at her, but it was the police officer who spoke, his tone dry. "It seems you have a character witness, Mr. Emerson. But perhaps she's somewhat prejudiced in your favor?"

Lauri blushed and let go of Mac's arms. "No, it's the truth. I swear."

"You'll need to," the officer said, nodding. "All right, if you'll go back inside?"

Lauri returned to her seat, and she heard him telling Mac to wait in the other room.

The first police officer came back with a can of soda and a package of snacks, and she sipped the caffeinated drink and ate some of the crackers as she told her story to two policemen. Early on, they asked her name and her mother's name and phone number.

"She—she works at the doctor's clinic on Juniper Street," Lauri told them, trying not to think of her mother's reaction to a call from the police.

One officer went to another office to phone, while Lauri continued with her story, repeating all the details carefully, slowly. Whatever happened to Lauri, whatever her mother said when she found out, this was for Jamey, and that was what mattered.

When she had finished, the policemen looked at each other, and one of them picked up the tape recorder that had recorded her story.

"I'll need to get this typed out; can you wait a few minutes?"

She nodded, and this time they both left the office.

Lauri felt drained. Would it work? Would what she had told them make a difference? Maybe it had been Jamey's teacher who had first alerted the authorities, but the teacher didn't know what Lauri did. Without her testimony, maybe Mac would have had a hard time proving his innocence. But surely they would listen if she told the truth, wouldn't they?

And just as important was the fact that Jamey would heal, would be okay; she still felt ashamed of having waited so long to act. Still, the thought of Jamey living among strangers made her want to cry—he was such a shy little boy. What if the foster parents didn't understand him?

In a moment, she heard someone in the hallway, and she looked up, expecting another policeman. But it was Mac, alone this time.

She jumped to her feet as he paused in the doorway. For a long moment, they stared at each other without speaking.

"I should have told you the truth," Lauri said at last. "I know you can't forgive me, but—"

She saw him visibly relax and he stepped into the office. This time when she trembled, his arms came up to embrace her, steady her.

"You came here to tell the police I wasn't guilty," he said very quietly.

"Of course," Lauri told him, gulping back the tears that once again slipped down her cheeks. "I mean, I was coming anyhow to try to get help for Jamey, but when I went to the park and heard that the police had picked you up—you're not under arrest?"

Her eyes widened as she looked up at him for answer.

He shook his head. "No. The police turned up at the park and wanted me to answer some questions, and I agreed to come in. It seems that when the hospital—and then the police—asked your uncle about the injuries, he told them he thought it had happened at practice, that it must have been me who'd hit Jamey."

Instead of blaming his baby-sitter, Uncle Jack had fingered Jamey's coach, one of the little boy's favorite people in the world.

Lauri looked at the lines of tension around Mac's eyes, saw the strain still evident in his expression. Even being suspected by the police wasn't much fun. And what would have happened to his chance for a college scholarship—all that talk about character references and good citizenship—if he were convicted of child abuse? It could have ruined Mac's life. It was all her fault. If she had acted more quickly, Jamey wouldn't have been hurt again, Mac wouldn't have been unfairly accused.

"I'm sorry," she said, dropping her gaze. "I should have acted sooner, for everyone's sake."

Mac would hate her forever.

But he still had his arms around her, and he leaned forward, kissing the top of her head.

"But you stood up for me," he said, his voice low. "Even when you had to accuse someone in your own family. I won't forget that, Lauri. Do you—maybe—feel something for me, after all?"

"Oh, yes," Lauri told him, lifting her head quickly. "Yes, yes!"

He grinned, and inside her, Lauri felt some of the weight of guilt lift.

"The police said I could go; I'll come back tomorrow and sign my statement. I was about to rush back to the park; I might get there before the game ends. Do you want me to wait here and lend you moral support?" Mac asked.

How could he be so understanding? Maybe because he was a genuinely nice guy, and maybe guys like that did exist. Lauri took a deep breath and shook her head. "No, go back to the park so—so everyone will see that you're not to blame. I don't want rumors going around. I'll be okay." She smiled, though it took effort.

Mac let her go, but gave her hand one last squeeze. "I'll call you, okay?"

She nodded and after he left, sat back down on the

plastic chair. Alone in the office, she stared through the window's half-opened blinds at the street outside and the cars and trucks that rolled past. She felt very tired, and she thought about Jamey, hoping his arm didn't hurt too much, hoping she could see him soon. It seemed a long time later when they brought the sheets of paper back and she signed her statements. Then the policeman left again, but they still hadn't told her she could go. Now what?

When she heard the door creak, Lauri looked up, expecting to see another police officer. Instead it was her mother who stood there, her mouth a thin line, gazing at her daughter with an expression that Lauri found hard to read.

Lauri jumped up, her mind a blank. She didn't know what to say. She swallowed hard, but her mouth felt dry.

"I'm sorry," Lauri said, at last, her voice very low. "I know I promised, but I—I had to do it."

Her mother moved forward quickly and put her arms around her. Lauri leaned against her mother's chest, her eyes shut, and almost didn't hear her mom's answer. She spoke softly, her voice trembling.

"No, Lauri. I'm sorry. Sorry that you had to be the one to do this—sorry that I let you down, let Jamey down."

Lauri took a deep breath, weak with relief that her mother wasn't angry. "You believe me? About Jamey, I mean?"

"When the police called me at work, I went straight across to the hospital before coming here. I saw Jamey."

"He's okay?" Lauri interrupted eagerly.

"He will be," her mother told her. "His left arm is in a cast, but he's in satisfactory condition. Once he was assured that his father wasn't with me, he seemed more worried about missing his ball game than anything else."

Lauri grinned for a moment, then said quickly, "It wasn't Mac, Jamey's coach. It wasn't him, Mom, I promise. It couldn't be Mac."

Her mother nodded. "I know. I've been selfish, Lauri, I realize that, about the money and the house. I just wanted so badly to keep the house—it felt as if we were safe there, I guess. But it wasn't only the money, there was more. I couldn't face the fact that my brother could do such a thing to his own son. But when I saw the marks on Jamey's poor little body—"

Lauri saw the tears well up in her mother's eyes, and she hugged her hard. "Oh, Mom, I know. I know."

They clung together for a few minutes, then her mother opened her purse and got a tissue, blowing her nose briskly.

"It was my place, my responsibility, to talk to Jack, to report the abuse. We'll do better by Jamey, I promise you. How would you feel about Jamey coming to live with us?"

"Really?" Lauri looked at her mother in surprise. "That would be great."

"Good," her mother said. "They try to place a child with a family member, I think, if he has to be taken out of the home."

"Do you think they'll let him stay with us?" Lauri asked anxiously.

"If we all go to family counselling together," her mother suggested. "I think that might help our chances."

Despite the fact that Mr. Dugan had already suggested

it, Lauri was startled. "All of us? You and me, too?"

"I think it might be a good idea," her mother said.

Lauri thought about Karen's comments, about her own irrational anger with Mac, and nodded slowly. Maybe it would be a smart thing to do.

"Then it depends upon whether the social workers recommend placing Jamey with us, and whether the judge agrees. I'll try my best."

For Jamey, Lauri thought. So Jamey could have some safety, some happiness, at last.

Her mother had to speak to the police, now, and it was dark by the time they walked out to the parking lot and drove to the hospital where Jamey was a patient.

On the way to the hospital, they talked about putting the house up for sale.

"Don't worry," her mother said. "There are some nice apartments a few blocks over. You—or Jamey—wouldn't have to change schools, at least."

Thankful for that much, Lauri nodded and blinked against one last tear—this time for herself, for the bedroom she loved, for the loss of her first real home. But apartments weren't so bad, as long as they were still together.

At the hospital, Lauri entered the elevator beside her mom, eager now to see Jamey. Thank goodness she was sixteen and old enough not to be barred from visiting by hospital rules. Another woman in the elevator car carried flowers, and their sweet scent filled the narrow space. Tomorrow, Lauri told herself, she would buy a new toy to bring to her cousin; right now she just wanted to see for herself that he was all right.

When they reached the second floor, her mother led the way to Jamey's room. A little girl slept in the first bed, with a woman sitting beside her, reading.

They found Jamey in the far bed, half-hidden behind a blue curtain.

"Lauri!" Jamey looked up eagerly when he caught sight of her.

Lauri rushed to hug him, careful of the arm in the white cast, propped up by two pillows. With his other hand, he was eating ice cream from a small container.

"Look, chocolate. They have a whole freezer full of ice cream here. The nurse told me," he explained, waving his plastic spoon.

Lauri found herself caught between laughter and tears of relief. Her voice shook a little when she said, "That's good. How do you feel? Does your arm hurt?"

"Yeah," Jamey said, matter-of-factly. "And I missed the game, Lauri." His face twisted for a moment.

"I know, what a bummer. I'm sorry," Lauri agreed, her throat still tight. "I'm sorry about a lot of things, Jamey."

The little boy reached down beside him. "But look, Mac came by after the game and brought me a trophy anyhow. Even though I wasn't there. He said I'm still a—a 'portant member of the team,' " Jamey repeated, patting the small brass-colored trophy that had been half-hidden in the sheets by his side.

"That's right," Lauri agreed, and she saw her mother nod.

Jamey looked at them both, as if picking up currents of half-understood emotion. "Am I going home now?" he asked, sounding anxious.

"I think you have to spend the night in the hospital, Jamey," Lauri's mother told him gently.

"My dad's not coming?" His eyes widened a little until Lauri's mom shook her head firmly.

"No."

"Oh." Relaxing, he went back to his ice cream, but then looked up at Lauri. "Do you have to go home now? Look, I have a TV. You could watch it with me." He gestured with his plastic spoon toward the set mounted on the wall and blinked suddenly, his voice wavering. "I just—it's sort of lonesome here, that's all."

Lauri picked up the tub of melting ice cream and set it back on the tray table beside the hospital bed, then wiped the smears of ice cream off his face with a paper napkin. "I can stay a while. In fact, I'll stay all night with you, Jamey, if the hospital will let me."

"Really?" Jamey brightened at once.

Lauri looked up at her mother in silent inquiry. Her mom reached out to pat Jamey's hair, then touched Lauri's cheek.

"We'll both stay," she suggested. "Let me go talk to the nurse. I'll be back in a moment."

She left the room, and Lauri sat down on the side of the bed, putting her arm around Jamey very carefully so she wouldn't jar his cast. He leaned against her and sighed happily.

"The hospital's okay, and the nurses," he said, pressing his face against her shoulder until his voice was half muffled. "But I missed you, Lauri. I'm glad you're staying."

"Me too. You won't be alone any more. You're going to be okay now, I promise," Lauri told him, realizing that she could finally believe her own words. "*We're* going to be okay."